BODYGUARD

Book 8: Traitor

Also by Chris Bradford

The Bodyguard series

Book 1: Recruit

Book 2: Hostage

Book 3: Hijack

Book 4: Ransom

Book 5: Ambush

Book 6: Survival

Book 7: Target

Book 8: Traitor

Chris Bradford

Philomel Books

PHILOMEL BOOKS
an imprint of Penguin Random House LLC
375 Hudson Street, New York, NY 10014

First American edition published by Philomel Books in 2018. Adapted from *Target,* originally published in the United Kingdom by Puffin Books in 2016.

Library of Congress Cataloging-in-Publication Data is available upon request.
Printed in the United States of America.
ISBN 9781524739379
10 9 8 7 6 5 4 3 2 1

American edition edited by Brian Geffen.
American edition design by Jennifer Chung.
Text set in 11-point Palatino Nova.

To Veronica Hurley,
a legendary librarian

WARNING: Do not attempt any of the techniques described within the book without the supervision of a qualified martial arts instructor. These can be highly dangerous moves and result in fatal injuries. The author and publisher take no responsibility for any injuries resulting from attempting these techniques.

"The best bodyguard is the one nobody notices."

With the rise of teen stars, the intense media focus on celebrity families and a new wave of millionaires and billionaires, adults are no longer the only target for hostage-taking, blackmail and assassination—kids are too.

That's why they need specialized protection . . .

GUARDIAN

Guardian is a secret close-protection organization that differs from all other security outfits by training and supplying only young bodyguards.

Known as guardians, these highly skilled kids are more effective than the typical adult bodyguard, who can easily draw unwanted attention. Operating invisibly as a child's constant companion, a guardian provides the greatest possible protection for any high-profile or vulnerable young target.

In a life-threatening situation, a **guardian** is the final ring of defense.

PREVIOUSLY ON BODYGUARD . . .

When young surf champion Charley Hunter rescues a boy from a deadly shark attack, she attracts more attention than she bargained for. Approached by the enigmatic Colonel Black, she's offered the opportunity to become a Guardian . . .

"You do realize I'm just a kid," she told the colonel.

"The best bodyguard is the one nobody notices," he replied. "That's why young people like yourself make exceptional bodyguards."

"But I thought all bodyguards were ripped, muscular guys. I'm a girl, in case you hadn't noticed."

"That gives you a distinct advantage."

During the grueling training she undergoes at Guardian Headquarters, however, Charley comes to question that "distinct advantage" . . .

"Did you *have* to strangle Charley till she blacked out?" cried Blake.

"Steve said don't hold back," Jason replied, his tone defensive. "Anyway, it was for her own good."

"How's that?"

"If she can't fight me off, what chance does she have against a real attacker? We're not playing games here, Blake. There are no second chances. If you get it wrong on an assignment, you'll be coming home in a body bag. I mean, what was the colonel thinking when he recruited a *girl*?"

But Charley's not someone to give in so easily. Overcoming the prejudice and her fellow recruits, she works her way up the ranks to become Guardian's star bodyguard . . .

Only now, after taking out an attacker in real life, did Charley realize she was no longer a victim—no longer the vulnerable girl she'd been when her friend Kerry was abducted.

Now she was a force to be reckoned with.

With her reputation growing, Charley is hired to protect Ash Wild, the world's newest teen sensation. But

keeping the young rock star safe on tour proves a difficult task . . .

The music stopped and Ash froze in a dramatic pose, one fist raised to the sky.

"In-de-structible!" he cried.

The red dot came to rest in the middle of his chest once more. Ash was oblivious to the threat as he basked in his fans' applause.

No more encores, thought Charley, recalling the ominous death threat.

With perhaps milliseconds before the shooter pulled the trigger, she dashed onto the stage.

Despite Charley's valiant attempts, a crazed fan is determined to end Ash's career permanently . . .

The ingredients had been bought easily and without suspicion. Sugar and a frying pan from the supermarket. Saltpeter from the fertilizer section of a garden center. A small flashlight bulb, a nine-volt battery, a relay switch and some electrical wire from a hardware store. Finally, a large can of Hurtle high-energy drink and a cheap digital watch from a gas station.

All the key components were now in place: a timer, a

battery, an igniter and an incendiary mix—small enough to conceal in a backpack.

The bomb was complete.

Ash Wild is not the only target on tour. Charley finds herself in the firing line too . . .

Charley knew the pap guy was trying to bait her, but she had to quash any rumors before they got out of hand and drew too much attention to her. "For the record, I'm *not* his girlfriend."

"Then . . . what are you?" panted Gonzo, struggling to keep up with the group.

"PR," replied Charley, and she raced on.

"And I'm Santa Claus!" he called after her.

And as if the death threats and bomb alerts weren't enough, the tour seems plagued with near-lethal accidents . . .

Out of the darkness, a large missile-like object plummeted from above. Charley glimpsed it only at the very last second as it flashed past the central screen. There was no time to react.

The spotlight dropped from the lighting rig like a meteor. It smashed into the stage right where Ash was standing. Knocked off his feet by the impact, he crumpled to the floor. The audience fell deathly silent as their idol lay motionless among the debris of shattered glass, splintered wood and twisted metal.

But these accidents have a deadly twist to them . . .

Ash's laptop pinged as a new message came in. A photo appeared in the browser window of Ash onstage, the blur of a falling spotlight just behind his head.

The caption beneath read:

Accidents don't just happen.

Charley's now in a race to unmask the killer in their midst, before it's too late. But how will she spot a killer in a crowd of 50,000 screaming fans?

1

"Cancel the gig," insisted the bassist. "In fact, the whole damn tour!"

"No. There's too much at stake," said Terry. "We risk losing millions."

"We risk losing our lives!" the bassist shot back.

The band, tour manager, Big T and Charley were all crammed into Ash's dressing room backstage at the Nationwide Arena in Columbus. Word had leaked out about the message on Ash's computer, and the band had been spooked.

"I tell you, it was an accident," insisted Terry. "Just because some anonymous hater posted a message online claiming he was responsible doesn't mean it's true. There's absolutely no evidence of foul play. This is simply an Internet troll taking advantage of a news story. Now get yourselves ready for the concert."

Charley kept her mouth shut. She no longer knew what

to think. Big T had launched an investigation into the source of the message, but it had so far come up blank. This was suspicious in itself. Yet an examination of the spotlight had pointed to basic mechanical failure of its clamp as the reason for the accident. The fact that the safety chain hadn't been attached was put down to human error, rather than a premeditated murder attempt. Nor had there been any reason to suspect the bus crash was anything more than an accident. However, following the ominous message, Charley began to wonder if that was really the case.

"Hey, it's not just Ash out there onstage," the bassist reminded them, crossing his arms defiantly. "Any one of us could be hurt or killed. So we have a right to say whether we go on or not."

"Fine," said Terry. "If you don't want the gig, we'll get another bassist in."

"Well, I hope he wears a crash helmet!" he sneered.

"Terry, you're missing the point," the drummer piped up. "We all know about the death threats. Someone has it in for Ash." He directed his drumstick at Ash, who sat mute in his chair, staring blankly at himself in the mirror as the stylist put the finishing touches on his hair. "Are you willing to gamble with his life, and ours, like this?"

"There is no gamble," said Terry. "I've discussed this with his manager. Someone is playing a cruel game, that's all. They're trying to scare Ash, intimidate him—sabotage his career. And we won't let that happen. Apart from the threats before the tour, it's all been false alarms. The crew has double-checked everything at this venue. I can assure you, there'll be no more accidents on this tour."

"That's comforting to know," replied the bassist. "But what about actual attacks on us?"

Terry jabbed a thumb in the direction of the veteran bodyguard. "That's the job of Big T and his security team to prevent—and I have complete faith that they'll keep Ash safe."

The bassist snorted. "That's all well and good for Ash. But what about *us*?"

"My security team covers you as well," said Big T.

Terry glanced impatiently at his watch. "Now, the gig's going ahead with or without you. What's it going to be?"

"Surely, it's *my* decision!" interrupted Ash. "Whether the show happens or not?"

Everyone in the room turned to him. Dressed in his glittering stage gear, his hair perfectly coiffured, Ash looked more than ready to go onstage. But, having seen him with his defenses down, Charley knew the paralyzing fear that haunted Ash's every waking moment. In her opinion, he was in no fit state to perform.

While the others in the band had a right to be concerned for their safety, Ash was the real target.

2

Pete was as jittery as any one of the twenty thousand Wildling fans packed into Columbus's Nationwide Arena. Perhaps even more so because he knew what was coming.

This time he'd managed to get a standing ticket and, after a fair bit of pushing and shoving, was in prime position right beside the neck of the guitar stage. The atmosphere in the arena was highly charged. After the tragic and abrupt end to the Pittsburgh show, Ash's fans were even more desperate to see him. Rumors had been flying that the concert would be canceled at the last minute, and a barely suppressed panic had spread among the audience. Some fans had even resorted to praying in groups for Ash's delivery onto the stage.

Thirty minutes later than scheduled, the house lights dimmed and the countdown began.

The audience screamed in delight. Pete enthusiastically joined in with the countdown, barely able to hear himself above the noise. His gut tightened as the opening explosion rumbled from the speakers, and he had to shield his eyes from the blinding cascade of red and gold sparks. His own heart seemed to beat in unison with the intro's rhythm. Then he felt a rush of exhilaration as the winged silhouette flitted from screen to screen before being consumed by flames.

INDESTRUCTIBLE . . . IMPOSSIBLE? . . . I'M POSSIBLE!

Ash shot up from the toaster lift and landed on the stage. *Not as perfectly as in New York,* thought Pete, *but still an impressive entrance.*

Immediately Ash took two strides forward before thrusting a fist into the air. "What's up, Columbus?"

The audience roared their approval, relieved and overjoyed to see their idol. After a swift, almost unconscious glance upward, Ash struck the opening chord to "Easier," and the band kicked in.

Pete sang along to every word. He watched Ash dance across the stage, his eyes never wavering from his idol. Even after a couple of shows, Pete was beginning to recognize some of his routines. But he could tell Ash wasn't as self-assured as in previous gigs. His performance seemed a little "tight," and every so often, the rock star would look nervously up at the lighting rig. That was to be expected, though, considering Pittsburgh.

Pete's arm started itching. He tried not to scratch the scabbing skin underneath the bandage; otherwise he'd damage his new tattoo.

Midway through the gig, a dark-haired girl with freckles stood on his foot. She was thirteen, maybe fourteen, and chewing gum voraciously. She shot him an apologetic smile, then did a double take. The girl opened her mouth and said something. But Pete couldn't hear her over the noise of the band and screaming fans. He leaned closer, and she shouted in his ear, "I said, you look just like Ash. Has anyone told you that before?"

"No," he replied, shaking his head.

"Well, you do!"

Pete grinned. He'd made an extra-special effort to resemble his hero. He'd even managed to find some clothes that matched the ones Ash wore. And it pleased him every time some fan mentioned the similarity.

All through the next set of songs, Pete was aware that the girl kept sneaking peeks at him. She'd "bump" against him, her bare arms touching his. With so many people crowded around, it was impossible not to be in contact with one another, but the girl seemed to be doing it on purpose. He caught her eye and responded with the Ash Wild trademark smile he'd been practicing every night in the mirror. She coyly looked away, but remained close.

As the girl continued to flirt with him, Pete thought to himself that he would *kill* to have Ash's life.

3

The Columbus gig proceeded without a hitch. Although the band knew that Ash's performance wasn't as slick as usual and a couple of times he missed his cues, his fans were too delirious to notice. Over the course of the following Louisville, Nashville and Charlotte dates, Ash's confidence gradually returned, and by the time the tour reached Atlanta, he was fully back on form—the spotlight incident little more than a bad memory.

But Charley hadn't forgotten. Nor had Big T. Security had been quietly stepped up, and everyone on the team was in a permanent state of Code Yellow. The tour schedule was punishing: early starts, late finishes and periods of mind-numbing inactivity followed by sudden bursts of chaos; long journeys, multiple locations and different hotel rooms every night. After only a week, Charley was shattered with the effects of tour fatigue. She became worried that in her exhausted state she might make another error of judgment, overlook a threat or simply not react in time to an attack. Thankfully, there had been no further incidents or threats made since Pittsburgh. But whether that was due to the security team's diligence or the fact that the maniac fan was biding his or her time, they didn't know. They simply had to stay alert, day and night, hour upon hour, minute by minute.

On arrival at the five-star Mandarin Oriental Hotel in Miami, Big T gave Charley her key card and a spare key card for Ash's suite. "Security-check his room, then get some rest," he ordered. "You look exhausted."

Leaving Big T to guard Ash, Charley headed up in the elevator and found his room. This time it wasn't ideally positioned at the end of the corridor. But they'd block-booked all the rooms surrounding Ash's to make the floor as secure as possible. Her room was opposite. She dumped her bags, then let herself into Ash's suite. The VIP room was as luxurious as ever, if not more so, with its dramatic views over the turquoise-blue waters of the Biscayne Bay.

She'd always wanted to visit Miami, and it certainly didn't disappoint: the colorful art deco buildings lining the sun-kissed streets, the pure white sand of the glorious beaches and the trendy surfside hotels packed with celebrities and wannabes. Sets of waves peeled along the coast, beckoning to her as surfers rode the white water in to the shore. Charley was itching to go out on a board herself but doubted she'd get the time on tour. Perhaps, she thought, she'd ditch the planned rest and go surfing instead. But first she had to security-sweep Ash's room.

Charley checked the bathroom, a spacious marbled affair with a freestanding tub and walk-in shower. Then she returned to the adjoining bedroom and opened the mirrored wardrobes.

"Did you lose something?"

Charley spun around to find Ash at the door. "No, just checking for groupies," she replied, echoing Big T's answer.

Ash laughed. "Now that *would* be room service!"

He strolled in, glanced at the king-sized bed swathed in soft linens and coral-colored throw cushions, then went to the window and peered out at the idyllic view.

"I haven't finished my security sweep," explained Charley. "It might be best if you wait in the lobby with Big T."

"Don't let me stop you," replied Ash. "I just needed to escape the madness downstairs."

"Does Big T know where you are?"

"No. But I'm with you, so I'm safe, aren't I?"

Charley thought about insisting that he leave. She knew the room wasn't technically safe yet. But, like Big T, she wasn't employed to tell Ash what he could or couldn't do. Besides, she was too tired to argue; she resumed her search.

"So, do you always have a key to my room?" he asked, raising an eyebrow as she looked under the bed, then opened the drawers to the bedside cabinets.

Charley nodded. "So does Big T. In case of an emergency." She pointed to the hotel map on the back of the door. "Speaking of an emergency, in case of fire, your nearest exit is to the right, five doors down."

"Boy, you must be a fun date!" said Ash, collapsing on the bed and scattering the carefully arranged cushions. "Don't you ever relax? Let your hair down?"

In recent days, she'd noticed Ash had returned to his usual flirtatious and slightly arrogant self. In fact, having bounced back from his low point, he was acting even a little hyper. She suspected he was still suffering from shock.

"Sure," Charley called from the lounge, "but not when I'm on an assignment."

"How many assignments have you done?"

"This is my sixth."

"Six! Who were the five before me?" he asked.

Switching on Big T's bug detector, Charley began a scan of the lounge's furnishings and fittings. "Sorry, that's confidential information."

"Well, have you protected anyone as famous as me?"

Charley rolled her eyes. "No, of course not," she replied, holding the detector over the phone. "But they were no less important."

There was a moment's silence, then Ash asked, "Did you keep them all safe?"

Charley thought about Sofia, the daughter of the Colombian minister. "They're all still alive, if that's what you're asking."

Having established the lounge was clear of surveillance devices, Charley slid open the door to the balcony and stepped out. The late-afternoon sun was warm on her skin, and the light sea breeze refreshing. The ocean was calling to her. She glanced down at the lineup of surfers bobbing on the water and longed to join them. A quick inspection of the balcony confirmed that it wasn't overlooked or easily accessible from another room.

Ash jumped from the bed and joined her. "Worried that ninjas are going to attack me? We're four floors up!"

Charley leaned over the rail and gazed down at the large oval swimming pool beneath, its waters glinting in the sunlight. "Just checking alternative escape routes," she half joked. "You might be able to jump into the pool as a last resort."

Ash looked over the balcony. "Well, there's only one way to find out."

Before Charley could stop him, Ash vaulted over the side.

4

"NO!" cried Charley, her heart stopping in her chest as Ash plunged to almost certain death. Gripping the rail so tightly that her knuckles went white, she stared after the diminishing body of the rock star. Images of newspaper headlines flashed before her eyes . . . ROCK STAR COMMITS SUICIDE . . . WILD LEAP ENDS IN TRAGEDY . . . accompanied by paparazzi photos of a broken body beneath a bloodied white sheet.

A second later, there was a distant splash and a fountain of white water. Ash surfaced and whooped with delight. He waved up to Charley. "What a rush! Your turn!"

Charley shook her head. "No way!" she shouted back.

"Come on! Live a little!"

Charley was sorely tempted by the challenge. But she knew it was utterly foolish. From four floors up and with several feet of patio to clear, there was a huge risk of missing the pool. You had to have a serious death wish to attempt it. Nonetheless, she found herself emptying her pockets, clambering over the rail and perching on the edge.

"Take a leap of faith!" cried Ash.

Summoning up the courage, Charley launched herself from the balcony. The wind whistled past her ears, her clothes flapping madly like a flock of starlings. For a moment the azure waters of Biscayne Bay filled her entire vision. It was beautiful. Then she glanced down and saw the patio rushing up toward her.

She wasn't going to make it.

Arms and legs flailing, she braced for a bone-crushing impact . . . Then, by some miracle, her forward momentum carried her over the pool. She hit the water hard. All the breath was knocked from her lungs. Her feet touched the bottom and she kicked herself back up to the surface.

"*Whoa!*" she cried, the tension and tiredness of the past week obliterated in a single mad leap.

"Awesome, Charley!" said Ash, swimming up and hugging her. "Don't you feel *alive*?"

Charley nodded, the adrenaline coursing through her veins. For the first time in a long while, she felt exhilarated and unburdened by life. "You're one crazy rock star!"

"And you're one crazy bodyguard," he shot back.

In that instant, their eyes locked and there was an undeniable spark. Charley had no idea whether the attraction was a result of their shared thrill-seeking experience or something deeper, but she reminded herself that was a line not to be crossed. A bodyguard should *never* get involved with a Principal. Besides, she had Blake to think about, didn't she?

"Hey, you two idiots! What do you think you're doing?"

They broke away from their gaze. A furious pool attendant stood at the edge of the pool pointing to a sign that read **NO DIVING!**

"Sorry," Ash replied. "Must have missed the sign on the way down."

The two of them swam to the side and clambered out. Dripping wet, they hurried back into the hotel and through the lobby. There was a burst of excitement as a group of fans behind a roped barrier spotted Ash.

Big T came thundering over. "I've been looking everywhere for you, Ash! Don't sneak off like th—" Then he noticed their soaking clothes. "What the hell have you two been up to?"

"We took a dip in the pool," replied Ash with a grin.

Big T gave Charley a hard stare, his eyes almost bulging from their sockets.

"Don't worry, I was with him the whole time," she replied, edging past the mountainous bodyguard to avoid any questions about how they'd ended up fully clothed in the pool.

Taking the elevator back to the fourth floor, they caught themselves in the mirror and burst into laughter at their bedraggled appearance.

"I still can't believe you jumped!" said Charley. "And that

I followed. You really scared me. That was an insane stunt, you know."

Ash shrugged. "Live fast, die young, eh?"

"Not too young, I hope," she said. "At least not while I'm protecting you."

Ash looked Charley up and down. "Seriously, could you *really* protect me?"

Charley's eyes hardened and her nostrils flared. Just as she was beginning to like him, he had to put his big foot in his mouth and question her ability as his bodyguard—simply because she was a girl.

"Don't take offense," said Ash, holding up his hands. "It's just by comparison to Big T, weight for weight, you don't look like you could pack the same punch."

Charley squared up to Ash in the lift. "Take a swing at me."

"What?"

"Come on! Punch me. I dare you to!"

Ash became visibly flustered. "No . . . um . . . I . . . don't hit girls."

Charley laughed. "Well, that's my first advantage in a fight," she replied. "Believe me, I pack a punch." She thrust her fist forward, lightning-quick, stopping just as her knuckles brushed the tip of his nose.

Ash flinched. "Okay, I believe you!"

The elevator pinged and the doors parted. Ash was only too eager to step out. Charley laughed at his swift retreat. As they turned down the corridor, a hotel employee in a maroon uniform was exiting Ash's room. He walked off in the opposite direction.

"Hey!" called Charley. "Can we help you?"

"Porter," explained the guy, not looking back. "Just brought up your bags."

The employee disappeared through a service door and down the stairs.

Surprised the man hadn't bothered to wait for a tip, Charley followed Ash into his suite. While he headed to the bathroom for a towel, she collected her phone and belongings from the balcony table, along with Big T's bug detector. She noticed she had a text from Blake asking her to call. The message was from his personal phone, so she knew it wasn't urgent or mission sensitive. But the two of them hadn't had a real conversation, one-on-one, in a while—the hectic tour schedule and the time difference making it hard for them to connect. When she was back in her room, she'd make sure to call him.

"Sorry for what I said in the elevator," Ash called out as she pocketed her phone. "I didn't mean—"

"Forget it," replied Charley as Ash flashed his charming smile through the open bathroom door. She found herself gazing at him, their eyes lingering on each other a little longer than necessary. A slight flush rose in her cheeks . . . *What's going on?* she thought. Ash wasn't even her type. She tried to get a grip on herself. "Listen . . . I'm just going to my room to find some dry clothes. I'll radio Big T to send up security."

There was a knock at the door.

Charley opened it. A man in a maroon uniform greeted her with a tip of his cap. "Sorry to disturb you. I'm Christian, the hotel porter. Does Mr. Wild have his bags?"

"Yes," she replied, indicating the two suitcases embossed with his initials on the luggage rack.

"Ah, good," said the porter, evidently relieved. "I was concerned they'd been misplaced. But it appears your team has done my job for me. Have a nice day."

5

"Did you get a look at his face?" asked Big T, sitting down opposite Ash and Charley in the suite's lounge area, his ample bulk filling the armchair.

Charley shook her head, her hair still damp and her wet clothes clinging to her body. "The first porter, or whoever he was, disappeared down the back stairs before we even got close."

"Rick, examine the hotel's surveillance footage," ordered Big T. The security guard nodded and headed for the elevator. "Have you noticed anything out of place in the room since you got back?"

Charley glanced around. "No, nothing obvious."

"Ash, has your luggage been tampered with?"

"Not as far as I can tell," he replied, sitting on the sofa, wrapped in a hotel robe.

"Well, until I give the okay, leave them be," instructed Big T, his tone firm. "Charley, did you complete the surveillance sweep before your unscheduled dip?"

Charley shifted uncomfortably under the bodyguard's hard gaze. She sensed the big man held her partly responsible for this breach of security. "Pretty much. The room was clean."

"Sweep it again. Top to bottom," he ordered.

"Can I get changed first?" she asked, the air-conditioning in the room chilling her to the bone.

"No," said Big T emphatically. "This takes priority."

Rising from the sofa, Charley picked up the bug detector and began a second inspection without argument. At the same time, Big T carried out a full physical search of the suite. He started with the two suitcases, checking the locks for damage and any signs of tampering before sifting carefully through the contents. Once satisfied with the cases, he looked and felt under the sofa and chairs, behind the cabinets, inside the wardrobes and every other item of furniture in the room.

With nothing better to do, Ash headed into the bedroom, threw himself on the king-sized bed, grabbed the remote and switched on the TV. He flipped through the channels to a classic rock show and turned up the volume.

"Good idea," Big T remarked to Charley as "Sweet Child o'

Mine" by Guns N' Roses blared from the speakers. "Anyone listening in won't hear a thing over this!"

Halfway through their rigorous search, Rick radioed up to Big T. Charley heard the conversation over her earpiece. *"The security manager reran the surveillance feed for the last hour. A uniformed man is seen heading down the staff stairwell at sixteen-oh-seven hours, but his face is obscured by a porter's cap. Then we lose him. Sorry, Big T, not much help."*

"Roger that," replied Big T. "Ask the hotel staff if they saw anyone suspicious or a new face on the team. You never know, we might get lucky."

Charley moved through to the bedroom. Guns N' Roses had given way to Nirvana's "Smells Like Teen Spirit."

"Find anything?" asked Ash, slumped against the pillows, his hands clasped behind his head.

"Not yet," Charley answered, waving the detector over a picture frame.

"I'm sure it'll turn out to be nothing," said Ash. "Reception probably told another staff member to bring up my bags and the head porter is angry he missed out on a fat tip."

"Let's hope that's the case," said Big T, entering the bedroom to the fading guitar distortion of Nirvana.

"We Built This City" by Starship began playing on the TV, and Ash made a face in disgust. "Oh, this has got to be the worst rock song ever!"

Looking through the drawers, Big T pulled out a TV remote. "Have you scanned this?" he asked Charley.

She nodded. He was about to return the unit to the drawer when Ash switched channels.

Big T frowned. "Hand over *that* remote," he demanded.

"Sorry, I didn't take you for a Starship fan," replied Ash, switching back channels.

"I'm not," said Big T, taking the suspect unit from Ash and examining it. As soon as Charley passed the bug detector over it, the detector vibrated and the indicator shot into the red.

"Bingo!" said Big T. He prized open the plastic casing to expose a SIM card, microphone and transmitter.

Ash stared in disbelief at the covert bugging device. "You can't be serious! That's James Bond stuff."

"Who do you think planted it? Gonzo?" suggested Charley.

"Him or another pap guy," Big T replied. "Whatever, someone is going to great lengths to keep tabs on Ash."

"Surely it's *illegal* to bug someone," exclaimed Ash, his tone turning angry. "Gonzo needs to be arrested for this!"

"There's no hard proof it's him," said Big T. "Besides, while unauthorized telephone tapping is illegal, bugs and covert cameras fall into a gray area of the law." He snapped the SIM card in half, then crushed the fake remote in his beefy fist. "That's one less bug to worry about. It's just a shame we can't do the same to the paparazzi outside."

Completing their surveillance sweep, they confirmed the suite was now clean.

"Are you absolutely certain?" asked Ash, still freaked out by the discovery. "I don't want strangers listening to my every word."

Big T nodded, then glanced at his watch. "You'd better freshen yourself up, superstar. We leave for the venue in an hour. Don't worry, your privacy is secure, and I'll post someone outside your door."

Charley returned to her own room, shed her damp clothes and jumped into a hot shower. As the water ran down her back and warmed her, she thought about the mysterious porter. Had Gonzo been responsible? Or was someone more sinister involved? It had been a bold tactic to impersonate a hotel employee and enter Ash's room. Why were they so determined to spy on Ash? Was it purely to listen in and get a news scoop, or did they have a more dangerous motive in mind? There were too many questions and Charley had no answers. But she did have one idea.

Charley dried herself, then clambered into bed and managed to snatch half an hour's rest before they left. On waking, she hunted through her go-bag for what she needed, then joined Vince outside Ash's suite. As the two of them waited for Ash to make his appearance, she casually leaned against the door frame and fitted one of the Intruder devices

Amir had given her. Positioned at knee height, the pill-sized white sensor was barely visible against the white paint.

If anyone tried to enter Ash's room while they were away, she'd be the first to know about it.

6

"Awesome gig!" Jessie gushed as Ash came offstage following his second encore at the Miami arena. "I especially liked the moment when you pulled that girl from the audience. She almost *fainted* in your arms."

Jessie gazed longingly at her idol, clearly wishing she'd been that girl. Charley didn't blame her. Almost every girl in the arena must have wanted to be serenaded in Ash's arms like that.

"Thanks," said Ash, swigging from a water bottle. "What did you think, Charley?"

"Probably your best gig yet," she agreed, though she knew from the sudden burst of radio chatter on her earpiece that the unplanned invitation of the fan onto the stage had thrown the security team into a minor panic.

As the road crew set to work packing away the instruments and dismantling the stage, Big T escorted Ash to his dressing room. Charley followed close behind and stationed herself outside his door. Once Ash had showered and changed, they prepared to leave the venue.

"Okay, scrum time!" Big T announced, then opened the stage doors.

Outside, hundreds upon hundreds of fans were packed like cattle behind metal barriers. They shrieked in ecstasy when Ash emerged, the noise louder than a dozen amusement parks. Charley stayed close with Big T, her eyes scanning the crowd as Ash worked his way along the line signing the fans' programs and smiling for countless selfies.

By now Charley was accustomed to the deafening screams and crazed antics of Wildling fans. But the task of protecting Ash in that earsplitting chaos had not become any easier with so many new faces. And every one had the potential to be the maniac who'd promised Ash *no more encores*.

One face did stand out in the crowd, though. One that was both a familiar and frequent presence in the signing line after gigs.

"Hey, Ash, over here! It's me, Pete!"

A few fans gazed curiously at the Ash Wild look-alike. But the rock star himself didn't hear the boy over the cacophony of screams. The superfan waved his program in a desperate bid to get Ash's attention, but they were already moving on. Charley felt a little sorry for Pete as his expectant smile slumped into a wounded sulk.

Then a pack of photographers, including Gonzo, vaulted the barriers and rushed toward Ash and his entourage. They scuttled around the rock star with their cameras clicking and flashing, a constant strobe of white lightning. As the pack pushed and shoved for prime position, a telephoto lens hit Ash in the head.

"Ow! Watch it," he cried as his baseball hat went flying.

"Keep back!" Big T growled, using his bulk to shift the cameramen out of their way.

A loud metallic *clang* caused Charley to turn on her heel. A barrier had toppled over, and the fans spilled onto the walkway, all madly trying to get their hands on Ash's lost hat. And when the rest of the barriers collapsed, hordes more fans surged forward.

"Time to make like a shepherd and get the flock outta here!" said Big T, his voice harsh in the security team's earpieces.

The PES team closed ranks and spearheaded Ash through the crowd toward the waiting SUV. But with every step, the crush of fans grew greater and the determination of the paparazzi intensified.

"Ash, look this way!" called a photographer, half blinding him with a blaze of flash shots.

Ash shielded his eyes and kept his head down.

"Why are you running, Ash? Scared of your own fans?" taunted another pap.

Gonzo bobbed up, his finger pressed on Auto-Shoot. "Any more *accidents*?"

Ash glared at the rat-faced photographer. "Stop bugging me!" he cried, flinging his water bottle at the man. The bottle struck the telephoto lens, spraying water everywhere. Paparazzi cameras flashed, capturing the moment.

"Hey! That's assault!" snarled Gonzo, unable to suppress his triumph at having antagonized the rock star. "That's assault with a weapon!"

"That's a good joke, Gonzo," said Big T. "Ash was being nice. Thought you could use a drink."

"I'll sue you for damages, Ash!" Gonzo shouted, ignoring the bodyguard.

Big T blocked the pap's path, then bent down to his ear level. "And I'll have you arrested for trespassing and illegal bugging," he hissed.

"Don't know what you're talking about," snapped Gonzo, waving his camera in Big T's face. "Look at this. It's ruined. Are you gonna pay for it?"

The bodyguard laughed. "Hope you've got insurance!"

Big T and his team fended off Gonzo and the rest of the paparazzi, insults flying thick and fast, while Charley continued to escort Ash toward the SUV. But more and more fans pressed in, slowing their progress to a crawl.

Charley's phone pinged and vibrated. Her first thought

was the Intruder. Had it caught someone sneaking into Ash's suite? Despite the crush, she managed to slip the phone from her pocket and glance at the screen.

But it was just a text message from Blake.

`Too busy with Ash to call?`

Charley swore under her breath. She'd forgotten to call him back! And he'd sent just one accusatory question, no *hey, how are you doing?* That didn't bode well. But she was in no position to reply to him now.

When Charley looked up, a tall boy had blocked Ash's path. With a cutoff T-shirt and gold chain, a buzz haircut and shadow of a mustache, he didn't look like the typical Ash Wild fan.

"You were eyeing up my girl," he accused.

Ash looked perplexed. "Sorry, was I?"

The boy nodded. "Pulled her onstage. You pumped-up little jerk!"

Without warning, the jealous boyfriend launched a fist at Ash's face. Ash stared at the approaching knuckles, frozen like a rabbit in headlights. A millisecond before the fist struck its target, Charley shoved Ash aside and deflected the punch with her forearm.

The boy glared at her. "Out of my way!"

As he tussled with her, he attempted to throw another wild punch at Ash. Left with no choice, Charley palm-struck him in the face. There was a crunch of bone and a spurt of blood as his nose broke under the impact. The boy staggered backward to the horrified squeals of the fans and the inevitable flash of the paps' cameras.

Stun, then run, thought Charley.

"Come on!" she said, hustling a shocked Ash into the SUV before it sped away.

7

How I'd like to shake that boy's hand. He attempted what I'm dying to do . . . punch Ash Wild's lights out!

I'd love to bust his perfect nose. Flatten it across his perfect face. Pound it until the blood flows freely over his perfect lips and dimpled chin.

Instead that boy got what Ash deserves. A broken nose!

Where's the justice in that?

And where did that blond girl suddenly spring from?

I've seen her around, of course. But I just thought she was a hanger-on. Another doe-eyed Wildling that had somehow wheedled her way onto the tour. A daddy's girl with connections in the music business.

But the speed at which she reacted to the attack on Ash was remarkable! Almost as if she'd been trained for it.

The boy had to be a head taller and twice as strong. Yet she took him down as if he were little more than a twig on legs. I mean, she blocked not just one, but two of his punches in quick succession.

Then she floored him with a palm strike to the face like she was Bruce Lee's daughter!

Ash's bumbling bodyguard had barely turned around before the whole incident was over.

There's something odd about this girl. Dangerous, even. I'll have to keep an eye on her. She could be a complication to my plans. She's already gotten in the way once. I can't let that happen again.

Still, the boy's attack must've been a shock to Ash. I can take pleasure in that. His face was definitely pale. He may have even peed himself with fright!

Of course, he'll get over it. Unfortunately.

But he'll get a bigger shock soon enough.

One that he won't recover from.

8

WILDCAT!

Fan Lashes Out to Save Rock Star

Many pop idols inspire devotion from their fans, but the followers of teen sensation Ash Wild take their duties to the max. When the English rock star was allegedly attacked by Miami resident Carlos Sanchez, 16, following a sold-out gig, a mystery blond-haired girl stepped to his defense.

Emma Hills, 15, saw the whole incident. "The girl came out of nowhere. She was like a ninja. Before you knew it, the boy was on the ground, crying about his nose being broken."

Sanchez insists, "I was the victim of a misunderstanding. The girl just lashed out at me."

But several eyewitnesses said that Carlos threw the first punch. According to Kelly Jackson, 14, "He was jealous that his girlfriend had been onstage with Ash and the idiot thought he was making a move on her. He went to punch Ash, but this girl stopped him. Never mess with a Wildling, that's what I say!"

The anonymous girl who came to Ash's rescue was seen disappearing into a vehicle with the grateful rock star. CelebrityStarz.net has contacted Ash Wild's management about the incident, but they've so far declined to comment.

Who is the mysterious Wildcat? And will she make another appearance?

A picture of Charley in midstrike accompanied the feature. It didn't show her face completely, her hair getting in the way, but it did illustrate the devastating impact of her palm strike. The boy's head was rocked back like a PEZ dispenser, with blood flying from his nose. The surrounding witnesses all wore stunned expressions, in particular Ash, who was staring at her in openmouthed astonishment.

More pictures and amateur video clips capturing the moment followed the article posted on the celebrity news site. The Internet was literally exploding with the story, and #Wildcat was topping the social media trends. Charley couldn't have drawn any more attention to herself if she'd tried.

As she sat alone in the rear lounge of the tour bus on its way toward their next destination, her phone rang.

"Charley, it's Colonel Black," spoke the terse voice.

She closed her eyes and braced herself for the reprimand. "You've seen the coverage, then?"

"Hard to miss," said the colonel. "You've done exactly what Steve warned you *not* to—gotten your face splashed all across the tabloid news! Need I remind you that any self-defense must be necessary, reasonable and proportional? That boy could have you arrested for assault."

"But he attacked first," protested Charley.

"That may be the case. But there's a fine line between acting in self-defense and breaking the law. What is deemed 'reasonable' in the eyes of the law is a matter of opinion. You must be seen to use the *minimum* force necessary. Busting a guy's nose with a palm strike is not the most subtle response."

"At least I didn't *punch* him," she responded tartly.

"I appreciate that you did what you considered necessary to protect Ash, but your actions have not only reflected badly on his public image, they've threatened to expose the whole Guardian organization. In future, I expect your responses to be *low* profile."

"Yes, Colonel," she muttered before signing off.

Charley put down the phone and held her head in her hands. She couldn't believe the colonel's reaction. What was she supposed to have done—sweet-talk the guy?

"Hey, Charley, don't sweat it," said Big T, lumbering into the lounge. "The colonel wasn't in your shoes at the time. He didn't have to make the snap decision that you did. Besides, the boy isn't pressing charges. Too many witnesses saw him strike first. And he's too ashamed to admit a girl decked him."

Charley sighed. "But I've blown my cover."

"No, you haven't. Everyone thinks you're just a fan. But you did step up to the plate. And that's what counts. I despise people who talk the talk but don't walk the walk when the time comes. You learn who's who in your own journey of life. And you're the real deal."

Charley was surprised and heartened by his support. "But the colonel's right," she admitted. "I should have put him in an armlock, stunned him, anything but hit him in the face in front of the press."

"You reacted on instinct. There wasn't time to think. If you had, Ash would have suffered a painful and embarrassing attack—one that could have damaged his rock-star looks permanently. That would have been a lot worse for his public image."

Big T pulled back the sleeve of his T-shirt and flexed the massive biceps of his right arm. A tattoo of a cruise missile bulged on his weathered skin. The words **DANGER:**

WEAPON OF MASS DESTRUCTION were etched inside the body of the missile.

"In my days as a bouncer, my right hook ended many arguments," he explained. "At one stage, this arm was so legendary, people called it TNT. I only ever needed to land one punch in a fight."

He unflexed his arm and rolled down the sleeve.

"But, over the years of facing violence, I've learned that size means nothing and that your voice is the greatest weapon. It can control a situation, it can calm a person down or it can incite a riot. You can throw an opponent off guard by speaking softly. Your voice can charm and persuade, threaten or placate. It's the solution to most problems we face as bodyguards. Only bring out the big guns as a last resort"—he cracked a smile—"like you did."

"They're still following us!" said Charley as their blacked-out SUV raced through the streets of downtown New Orleans. They'd barely made it to their vehicle after the sold-out concert at the Superdome. Some eighty-five thousand fans had crammed in to see Ash perform, and seemingly almost as many had waited to catch a glimpse of him leaving with the now-infamous "Wildcat."

"Can't you go any faster?" asked Ash, peering through the rear window at the eleven cars, three scooters and two motorbikes that pursued them.

"I have to obey the speed limit," replied Shane, their driver, gritting his teeth in concentration.

"*They're* not!"

From the front passenger seat, Big T eyed their pursuers in the wing mirror. "Paparazzi pay no regard to road rules."

As if to confirm this, a rented SUV sped up the wrong side of the street as the cameraman jockeyed with the other pap vehicles for the best position. A car coming the opposite way blared its horn and the cameraman swerved at the last second to avoid a head-on collision.

"Isn't this how Princess Diana died?" exclaimed Ash, clinging to his seat as their SUV rounded a corner at speed.

"Buckle up, and you'll be fine," Big T told him.

Behind, the paparazzi motorcade scrambled to follow them—overtaking and swerving, speeding and blocking one another, anything to stay close.

Coming to a stop at a junction, their SUV was swamped by vehicles and was almost boxed in. Photographers leaned out of their windows and filmed and photographed whatever they could. The lights changed. Shane forced his way through the blockade, and the chase resumed.

Ash sighed. "Don't they ever give up?"

"They're like vampires," grunted Big T. "Whatever they get is never enough."

Their SUV passed through an intersection just as the traffic lights turned red. Behind them car horns blared and there was a screeching of tires. As the convoy of paparazzi ran the red light, two vehicles collided, blocking the junction.

Charley had never experienced anything like it. The chase was straight out of a Hollywood movie, except that real lives were at stake. And all for a sleazy celebrity photo!

Turning onto the freeway, Shane was able to put his foot down on the accelerator at last. He weaved in between the traffic, trying to put some distance between them and the relentless paparazzi. But it was futile. Without breaking the speed limit and risking the lives of his passengers, Shane was limited in what he could do to shake off their pursuers.

At the last possible moment, he took the off-ramp to their hotel. Three vehicles in the outside lane were too late to make the exit, but the remainder of the unwanted motorcade funneled down the ramp and back into the city.

As they neared their hotel, a motorbike came up alongside, the rider brandishing a camera. Hardly looking where he was going, he pressed the lens to the front windshield and ran it on full auto. The multiple flashes lit up the darkened interior of the car like a magnesium flare.

The driver instinctively held up his arm to shield his eyes, but he was already blinded by the glare. He swerved, hit the curb, bounced back into the road, then veered off.

Big T had just enough time to shout, "Brace yours—" before the SUV hit a lamp post. Ash and Charley were flung forward, their seat belts jerking them to a violent stop. The airbags in the front saved the driver and Big T.

For a moment just the hiss of the SUV's radiator could be heard. Then Big T broke the silence: "Everyone all right?"

Charley's heart was pounding hard, her hands trembling. She felt bruising where the belt had dug into her ribs, and it hurt to breathe, but she didn't think anything was broken. She gave Big T a thumbs-up, then looked over at Ash. He appeared dazed, and blood was running from a cut above his left eye.

"You okay?" she asked.

Ash met her gaze and nodded. She quickly inspected the cut. It was superficial, caused by a glancing blow to the side window. She noticed some bruising, indicating a chance of concussion, but Ash's eyes were focused and he seemed only to be in shock.

Through the windshield, Charley spotted the helmeted motorcyclist responsible for their crash. To her disgust, he took several photos of their disabled SUV before racing away from the scene. Around them, the other paparazzi discarded their vehicles on the roadway and swooped like vultures on the accident.

"Shane, you stick with the car until the cops turn up," ordered Big T. "Charley and I will get Ash to the hotel."

As the three of them emerged from the wrecked SUV, they were assaulted by a hailstorm of camera flashes.

"Ash, you're hurt!" cried one photographer, not with concern but glee at the chance to get a dramatic shot. He shoved the camera in Ash's face to snap away at the blood seeping from his cut.

"Who was driving?" another scruffy photographer asked. "Are you responsible, Big T? Or Wildcat here?"

Big T pushed through the ring of cameramen, brushing

them firmly aside. He kept an arm around Ash, ensuring his charge remained steady on his feet.

"Ash, I thought Wildcat was your bodyguard now," teased a pap.

Big T scowled at the man and pushed him from their path.

"Ooh, touchy!" taunted the pap. "Worried you'll be out of a job? You're pretty old for this game, aren't you?"

Big T turned sharply on the man. "Want to meet my *old* fist?"

Surprised to see her mentor losing his cool, Charley urged the veteran bodyguard on. "Ignore the idiot," she hissed. Taking Ash's arm, she helped escort the dazed rock star toward the hotel entrance.

Gonzo suddenly appeared amid the pack, eyes gleaming. "Does she hold your hand at night too, Ash?" he goaded with a grin.

Charley had wondered where the despicable rat had been all this time. The taunts wouldn't have been the same without him. Ignoring the loaded question, she headed for the sanctuary of the hotel with Ash and Big T. Cameras continued to hose them down with flashes as they were heckled every step of the way. Charley found it hard not to respond to the offensive comments, but she knew that any answer she gave would only stir them up more.

Bundling Ash through the hotel doors, they left the hungry paparazzi in the street. Cameras flashed through the glass, and their taunts, though muffled, could still be heard.

Charley glanced back at the mob of photographers. How was she expected to keep a low profile now?

10

"So there you have it, folks," said the TV show host, flashing her crystal-white smile at the camera. "Ash's guardian angel wasn't just a fan, after all. The Wildcat, as we've all come to know her, was a PR intern on his team. It seems that protecting a rock star's image nowadays takes more than the ability to type up a press release. You have to be a ninja!"

A picture of a black-hooded assassin flashed up on the studio monitors, and the sound of clashing swords and the shouts of *kiai* were overdubbed.

Charley stood off camera with Big T and Zoe, watching Ash's interview from the darkened wings of the recording studio in Dallas, Texas. Kay had agreed with Zoe's suggestion that their best PR strategy was a straight exposure of Charley by Ash on national TV. This, they all hoped, would bury the story, and the news agencies would move on to the next celebrity scoop.

Charley felt her phone vibrate in her pocket. She glanced

at the glowing screen. Following the porter incident in Miami, she now routinely fitted an Intruder device outside Ash's hotel room, so she thought it could be a surveillance alert. But it wasn't. It was a text from Blake:

`Can you talk?`

Outside the official report-ins, it was always difficult to find time to chat, and Charley sensed something was on his mind. She thumbed a reply:

`Can't speak now. In TV studio. Will call later. Promise`

The host swung her beaming smile back toward Ash and concluded her interview. "Thank you for coming into the studio, Ash. I'm glad the paparazzi didn't run you off the road like they did in New Orleans. And good luck with the concert tomorrow. I hear it's sold out!"

"It sure is!" Ash replied with enthusiasm, the cut above his left eye now healing and hidden by makeup. "I can't wait to see all my Dallas fans go WILD!"

"Well, judging by the crowd outside our studios, they can't wait to see you either. Now, I believe you're going to play us out with your biggest hit, 'Only Raining.'"

Ash nodded, then joined his band on the opposite side of the studio. The cameras moved in for a close-up as he began the opening riff to his worldwide smash.

Charley found herself bobbing her head in time to the music. As Ash sang, *"We all need a shelter to keep us from the rain . . .*" her thoughts drifted back to the moment on the beach in California when she'd decided to catch that once-in-a-lifetime wave and become a bodyguard. How her life had changed—from being a surfing beach bum to protecting one of the most famous teenagers on the planet! And, though being a bodyguard wasn't easy, her life no longer felt empty or without purpose. Yes, Kerry was still a huge hole in her heart, but the memory only stung . . . It didn't burn anymore. For that she was thankful. She just wished her parents could've been around to witness this. But if they had been, of course, she'd never have become a bodyguard in the first place.

Charley became aware of someone at her side. Glancing over, she did a double take: same quiff of honey-brown hair, identical hazel eyes, dimpled chin, a matching smile. Standing next to her was a carbon copy of Ash.

"How did you get in here?" hissed Charley, suddenly realizing who it was.

"The receptionist thought I was Ash!" The clone laughed quietly. "Look, I've even got the same tattoo now."

Pete pulled back the sleeve of his shirt to reveal an identical phoenix design on his right forearm.

"You really shouldn't be here," insisted Charley.

"I know," he said with a charming smile he'd stolen straight from Ash, "but I wanted to see what a TV studio was like."

The band brought the song to an end and, after thanking Ash, the host made her closing remarks. As the studio's red recording light switched off, the producer announced, "Okay, everyone, we're off the air."

"Excellent interview, Ash, and even better performance," praised Zoe, handing him a bottle of water as she led him from the set.

"Thanks," said Ash, lifting the bottle to his lips. But he didn't get any farther with his drink, literally stopped in his tracks by the sight of his double.

"Hi, Ash! Check out my tattoo," said Pete eagerly.

Ash glanced at it. "Nice tat. Is that real?" he asked in astonishment.

"Of course!" Pete said, grinning.

Ash continued to study his apparently identical twin, as if looking in a mirror. "You're . . . *me*!"

Big T came striding over and, after a momentary blink of disbelief, immediately took charge. "I'm going to have to ask you to leave," he said firmly to Pete.

The doppelgänger held up his hands. "Hey, Big T, I'm no threat to Ash. I *idolize* him."

"That's more than apparent," said the veteran bodyguard, stony-faced. "But you'll still have to go. This is a restricted area."

"I understand," said Pete, shrugging his shoulders as two

studio security guards appeared. "See you at the gig tomorrow night, Ash."

"Yeah," said Ash, still shocked by his fan's devotion. As the guards escorted Pete away, Ash whispered to Charley, "Don't tell him, but he's got the tattoo on the wrong arm!"

Charley stifled a giggle—the poor boy, after the lengths he'd gone to in mimicking his hero. He'd likely be even more dismayed when he discovered that Ash's tattoo was just temporary.

"Sorry about that," said the producer, running over. "I'll be having a word with our security manager later. But first let's get you on your way."

The producer guided Ash and his entourage out of the studio and down the corridor. Turning a corner toward the reception desk, they caught a glimpse through a window of the heaving throng of photographers and fans packing the studio's plaza entrance.

"This is ridiculous," said Zoe. "We can't even get out to the car!"

Following the assault in Miami and the crash in New Orleans, the paparazzi had intensified their pursuit of Ash and his Wildcat. It seemed every photographer in the United States had descended on the tour, and it was now a challenge just to reach the venues, let alone keep Ash safe.

"We could try the emergency exit," the producer suggested.

A squeal of excitement in the lobby caught their attention. An intern had spotted Pete being escorted away and rushed over for his autograph. Pete signed the girl's notepad with a flourish, the two security guards barely able to contain their amusement at the case of mistaken identity.

"I have a better idea," said Ash.

11

Sunglasses on, Ash emerged from the TV studio into the teeming plaza. The crowd erupted with screams and surged forward. A strobe of camera flashes lit up his exit as the paparazzi swarmed around their target. With his arm protectively over the shoulders of the young rock star, Big T forged a path through the ocean of hysterical fans and in-your-face photographers. The rest of Ash's entourage followed in his slipstream.

It took almost ten minutes to reach the car, even though it was parked only fifty yards away. Unwilling to disappoint his fans, Ash spent time signing autographs and posing for numerous selfies. Eventually Big T bundled him into the back of the car and they drove away from the studio. The paparazzi immediately piled into their vehicles and set off in hot pursuit.

Their idol gone, the fans dispersed and the plaza emptied.

"That worked like a dream!" said Ash, emerging from behind the reception desk with Charley.

"Pete certainly lived up to his role," agreed Charley. The plan had been that Pete would go straight to the car with Big T, but the boy had obviously been swept up in the thrill of adulation and exploited his sudden stardom to the max.

"I'll have to employ him full-time as my decoy," continued Ash. "I'll get Big T to give him a backstage pass."

Charley frowned. "Are you sure that's wise? You hardly know him."

Ash laughed. "Of course I know him. He's me!"

Charley gave him a hard look. "Seriously, Ash, what normal fan goes so far that they get the same tattoo as their idol?"

Ash waved away her concerns. "Thousands of people copy their heroes. Girls are always imitating their favorite pop stars. Why should it be any different for a guy? Pete is just super dedicated. And if he can fool the paparazzi, then I'm all for it."

"We should at least run a background check on him," insisted Charley.

"Fine, whatever. But look outside." He pointed to the deserted plaza. *"No paparazzi!"*

He grabbed Charley and did a little jig in the lobby. Charley couldn't help smiling. His joy was infectious, and she too felt a weight lift from her. The constant surveillance and taunts had made her more tense than she'd realized. It would be a welcome change to walk outside without cameras being thrust in her face.

"Your car's here," announced the receptionist.

Ash danced his way through the revolving doors as a second vehicle drove up to the studio entrance. Charley followed him out and jumped in the back with him.

"Time to celebrate my newfound freedom." Ash tapped the driver on the shoulder. "Take us to the best restaurant in Dallas."

"Big T said we should go straight to the hotel," Charley reminded him.

"Come on, Charley, live a little! Besides, what could possibly go wrong? I've got the Wildcat to protect me!"

12

"I'm sorry, sir, we're fully booked for dinner," the bow-tied, straightlaced maître d' at the door of the ultra-chic restaurant in downtown Dallas informed them. His hair was a splash of oil slicked to his scalp, his hands manicured to a high sheen and his shoes polished to within an inch of their lives.

"But I can see a free table in the window," said Ash.

"That's reserved for special guests," the maître d' replied haughtily. "Perhaps I can recommend the burger bar down the street?"

Ash ignored the man's snub. "How special do you need to be? I'm Ash Wild."

The maître d' looked down his thin nose at him. "And who's he?"

"*Who's Ash Wild?*" exclaimed a gruff voice from behind a velvet curtain that separated the restaurant's entrance from the dining area. "Only the greatest songwriter since McCartney!"

Pushing through the curtain, the head chef, with flushed cheeks and a reassuringly ample belly, bowled over to greet Ash with a warm handshake. "My word, it *is* you! My daughters loves your music. And I must admit I'm a real fan too. Just adore 'Only Raining'! I was so disappointed when I couldn't get tickets for your concert. But you've come to *my* restaurant, and it'd be an honor to cook for talent like yours."

"Why, thank you," said Ash, startled by the gushing praise. "I'm sure that my publicist can arrange tickets for you and your daughters."

The chef's face lit up. He turned to his maître d'. "Show Ash to the best table in the house," he ordered.

"My apologies, Mr. Wild," said the maître d', a bald patch gleaming in the spotlight as he bowed his head. "I don't keep up with modern music."

"No, I'm sure you don't," said Ash politely.

The maître d' led them through the curtain and over to the table by the window. He drew back the chair for Charley.

"We can't sit here," Charley said to Ash, still standing.

"Why not?" he asked with a puzzled frown. "This is the very best seat in the house."

"The very best seat is often the worst from a security point of view."

Ash looked out of the window. "But we've got a great view over the park."

"That's the problem," said Charley, lowering her voice.

"It makes you vulnerable. Anyone could spot you or"—she thought back to the laser at the first gig—"attack you."

Ash stared at her. "Wow, you make for a romantic dinner date!"

Charley tilted her head. "I didn't know this was a *date*."

Ash glanced at the red rose decorating the table, then met her eye and smiled. "Neither did I."

"Mr. Wild, is this table not suitable?" inquired the maître d', raising a needle-thin eyebrow.

"It's perfect," replied Ash, and sat down. "Listen, Charley, no one knows we're here, so let's just enjoy this moment of rare freedom."

Charley reluctantly took her seat, but positioned it so that she at least had a view of the other restaurant guests. Besides, it wasn't quite true that no one knew where they were. She'd texted Big T an update of their location while Ash had been speaking with the head chef. She certainly wasn't going to make the same mistake twice with the veteran bodyguard.

The waiter came over with a bread basket, poured them some chilled water and presented the menus. There was a ripple of excitement among the other diners and staff as word spread of their special guest.

"So what other security advice should we be following?" asked Ash as he browsed the menu.

"Well, we should have our backs to a wall," replied Charley.

"Then we only have to worry about threats from the front. Also, it'd be better if I had a direct line of sight to the restaurant entrance and any other doors. That way I can keep an eye on who comes in and who goes out."

Ash set aside his menu. "They taught you all this in bodyguard school?"

Charley nodded. "Among other things."

"Like how to deck a guy with a single punch!"

"It wasn't technically a punch," replied Charley, sipping her water. "It was a palm strike."

"Whatever, you laid that idiot out," said Ash, grinning at the memory. He leaned forward, elbows on the table, his fingers interlaced as if in a confession. "I haven't thanked you properly for protecting me. The guy blindsided me. I just never expected it."

"No one ever does."

"But you did. You reacted."

"I've been trained to," said Charley. "It's all part of the job."

"Some job!" remarked Ash, shaking his head in amazement.

A waiter approached and took their orders.

"To be honest, I thought having you around was going to be a real drag," Ash admitted once the waiter had gone. "And, after that first gig, I had serious doubts about you. But . . . you're one amazing girl, Charley."

He gazed at her across the candlelit table, his smoldering hazel eyes both sincere and irresistible. Charley felt that spark again, and her pulse raced. Trying to keep her runaway emotions in check, she selected a bread roll from the basket and began to butter it.

"Don't get slushy on me," she said. "I'm your bodyguard. Not your girlfriend."

"I know, but it's really nice having you around," Ash admitted. "If I haven't said it before, I'm sorry for the tour prank we played on you. It was the bassist's idea. I didn't think you'd—"

"Forget about it. I have," said Charley, glancing up with a smile.

"Well, I haven't." Ash held her gaze as he took a sip of water. "Being a rock star isn't all it's cracked up to be," he confessed. "Everyone just sees the riches, the fans, the celebrity lifestyle. But life on the road can be so lonely."

"You've got the band around you," Charley pointed out.

"The band and crew are all friends, of course. But it's different—they're older. They're not going through what I am as the frontman. They don't have to contend with the pressure of fame . . . the haters . . . or the death threats. You see all that. You understand it. I can talk to you about it."

"Of course you can," said Charley.

Ash pulled out his phone, thumbed an app and showed her his social media feed on the screen. "This is what I have to put up with every day, every minute of my life."

He pointed to a post that read *Drop dead, you talentless waster!*

Another below it declared *Your music is an insult to anyone with ears.*

There were several other messages of abuse and threats to harm the rock star. But, as Charley had noted before, the majority of the posts were from loyal and loving fans:

```
I adore u @therealAshWild

So Xcited, #AshWild Dallas gig tm night!

Hoping for an *electrifying* performance! #AshWild

@therealAshWild has the voice of an angel.
```

Charley drew Ash's attention to these. "This is what you should be reading. Not those other insults. Ignore the haters. If you don't, they win."

Ash sighed. "I know, but that's easier said than done, especially when one of them could be the maniac who's trying to kill me."

Their conversation was interrupted by the arrival of their first course. Ash was presented with a plate of roasted maple-glazed buffalo wings, while Charley had chosen king prawns in a coconut mayonnaise. With a flourish, the waiter laid the napkins on their laps, then departed.

"Anyway, enough about my problems," said Ash, tucking into his starter. "You still haven't told me why you became a bodyguard."

Since Ash had opened up to her, Charley felt she could do the same. As they ate, she told him about Kerry, about the bald-headed abductor and how she'd failed to react and save her friend, then how her parents had died in a plane hijacking and her life had lost all meaning.

"They say time heals all wounds," mused Charley. "But, if that's true, the memories still leave a scar."

Suddenly she realized Ash was texting on his phone under the table. "Sorry, am I boring you?" she asked, her tone sharp.

"No, absolutely not. You're inspiring me!" he replied, rapidly typing away. After a minute or so, he put his phone down and sighed with deep relief. He gazed at her in awe. "Charley, I know you'll think I'm just flirting, but you're my missing muse. I've been stuck, fishing for lyrics, for weeks. Now I can hear the songs again—thanks to you."

Leaning closer, he sang softly to her, a heartachingly beautiful melody: *"Time will heal, yet memories scar, when the hurt's so deep, a bridge too far . . ."*

Charley felt her eyes moisten and her throat constrict.

"In times of trouble, I need a helping hand. I look for you, breathe for you, have a need for you . . ."

The words and tune combined to squeeze at her heart, the song seeming to be a distillation of her enduring grief. A tear escaped and rolled down her cheek. Still singing, Ash reached out with his own hand, gently caressed her face and wiped away the tear.

A sudden flash lit up the scene. Ash jerked his hand back. Charley blinked in half-blinded surprise.

Outside the window, grinning like a kid in a candy store, was Gonzo.

13

"It's not what it looks like," protested Charley over the phone the next morning.

But Gonzo's photo was compromising in every way—the candlelit restaurant, a red rose on the table, and Ash with his hand cupping her face.

From the angle the photo had been taken, it appeared the famous rock star was about to kiss her. And the camera never lies.

Charley stared in dismay at the image now making the front page of every tabloid and celebrity newsfeed in the world. "Wild Boy Tames Wildcat" and other puns accompanied the picture that had been published within hours of their dinner.

"Yeah, you're just doing your job," said Blake flatly. "It's good to see you're so committed."

"For heaven's sake, nothing happened. Please don't get jealous."

"How can you expect me *not* to be jealous?"

"I expect you to trust me," pleaded Charley.

"Well, that's a little hard, considering the evidence," he replied frostily. "And you rarely return my calls. You're obviously too busy with Ash. I think we should end it, don't you?"

Charley couldn't speak; Blake had been her friend since she'd joined Guardian. He'd been the one to stand by her when all the others had doubted her abilities. She didn't want to lose him, not like this.

But before Charley could manage a reply, he dropped another bombshell.

"Anyway, I was only going out with you because I felt sorry for you as the only girl in Guardian. But now there are others."

"What?" exclaimed Charley, but he'd already ended the call. For a moment she sat staring at the phone still in her hand. Then she picked up the newspaper with the offending photo and flung it across her hotel room. It hit the opposite wall, its pages scattering like autumn leaves.

"I warned you the paparazzi could make your life difficult," said Big T, leaning his great bulk against the door frame to her room.

Her vision swimming with tears, Charley sobbed, "Blake dumped me because of it!"

Stepping into the room, Big T wrapped a heavy, tattooed

arm around her shoulders to comfort her. "Then the boy's an idiot. He has no idea what he's lost."

"H-he says he only went out with me . . . b-because he felt sorry for me!" said Charley, her voice hitching.

Big T scowled. "Then he's a double idiot! Soon enough he'll realize his mistake and start feeling sorry for *himself*."

"Why would he even say that?" asked Charley.

"He's a boy. His pride's been hurt. It sounds to me like a cheap shot to have the last word."

Charley looked up, red-eyed and pleading at Big T. "But I didn't do anything with Ash."

"I know," said Big T with a sympathetic smile. "But bodyguarding and boyfriends don't mix, I'm afraid. There's little room for relationships in this line of work. I should know. I have two ex-wives!" He gave a hollow laugh.

"None of this would have happened if it hadn't been for that photo!" Charley ground her teeth, her sorrow now replaced by anger. "How did Gonzo find us?"

Big T shrugged. "Most likely an informant in the restaurant itself. Pap agencies spend literally hundreds of thousands of dollars a year on their snitch network. It's hard to keep any celebrity's movements secret these days."

"But wasn't he fooled by Pete?"

"Yes, hook, line and sinker," said Big T. "Gonzo followed us all the way back to the hotel. He staked out the entrance with everyone else. The only way he could have known you were at that restaurant was a tip-off. And whatever he paid the snitch, it's nothing compared with the small fortune he's raked in selling that single photo of you two."

Charley clenched her fists in frustrated fury; while she suffered the consequences of the lie, that leech had profited. "Well, he'd better leave us alone now."

"Fat chance. They're vampires, remember?"

Charley's phone rang. It was Colonel Black. She braced herself for another reprimand.

"Charley, this *isn't* what I meant by keeping a low profile," he began, his tone surprisingly even and restrained. "But I suppose it was inevitable. You can't protect one of the most famous pop stars in the world without attracting attention yourself. I just need to know, has a line been crossed here?"

"No, of course not," she replied.

"Good. If that's the case, then stay on the assignment, for now at least."

"Thank you, Colonel," she said, relieved simply to have escaped a shameful dismissal. Besides, after her messy breakup with Blake, she didn't want to go back to headquarters anytime soon. "I assure you it won't happen again."

"No, I'm sure it will," Colonel Black corrected her, much to her astonishment. "Kay and I are both in agreement. Considering the circumstances, being Ash's girlfriend is the perfect cover."

14

"There are literally millions of girls who'd kill to be in your position . . . me included," said Jessie, giving Charley a brief congratulatory hug when they met at the side of the stage for Ash's Dallas concert. "Ash always had eyes for you, so I'm not really surprised. You two are a match made in heaven."

"Well, it was certainly a surprise to me," Charley replied with an awkward smile. She was still reeling from her breakup with Blake. *How could he be so heartless?* She'd tried calling him, but he refused to answer his phone—his determined silence as hurtful as his sudden dumping of her. However, becoming Ash's official girlfriend overnight was an even greater shock to the system. Suddenly everyone wanted to know her—fans and paparazzi alike.

There'd been a huge explosion of online chatter and gossip about the blossoming romance. More of Gonzo's pictures had been released: early shots of the two of them leaving the after-show party in New York; the time they'd sneaked out of the hotel in Pittsburgh to go running; the now-infamous moment she'd leaped to Ash's defense; the anxious seconds after the car crash in New Orleans and other random shots from the rest of the tour. Ignoring any timelines or contexts, the press had created a whole fiction around the photos—a celebrity story of young love seen through the tabloid lens of the paparazzi.

GUARDIAN ANGEL TURNS LOVE ANGEL . . .

ASH RUNS WILD WITH NEW GIRL . . .

PR INTERN CAPTURES ROCK STAR'S HEART . . .

Investigative reporters had tried to dig up dirt on Charley, some even resorting to fabricating lies about her past, but Charley knew the press wouldn't find anything on her. Besides her last name being changed for the assignment, the personal records of all Guardian recruits were meticulously doctored to conceal their double lives as young bodyguards. This was for the security of the Principals as well as the recruits.

But the past wasn't as interesting as the present for the celebrity-hungry masses. Besides the big question of whether it was true love or not, Charley's looks were a huge subject of debate among girl fans—her blond hair, her sky-blue eyes, her slim neck, her athletic figure, her teeth, her nails, her taste in clothes. There was no part of her body or image not dissected and commented upon.

The Internet was teeming with these posts and, against her better judgment, Charley had read some. She couldn't stop herself. Skimming the comments, she was relieved to discover many opinions were flattering and supportive. But there were also a lot of spiteful remarks and cruel barbs. Some had been deeply personal and truly hurtful. Even though Charley realized they were written by trolls—bullies who only wanted to offend and humiliate—she couldn't help feeling upset at the unjust and unwarranted abuse. Many fans wrote that they hated her and she didn't deserve to be Ash's girlfriend. Some wished her dead. A few even threatened to kill her if she hurt Ash or broke his heart.

After a miserable hour of Internet surfing, Charley forced herself to stop. Like poison, the hate infected all the fan forums and dominated her thoughts, sending any nice remarks into oblivion. Charley's sense of self-worth was becoming seriously undermined. She was having a taste of Ash's celebrity life, and she didn't like it one bit.

Pete, on the other hand, was relishing his role as Ash's decoy.

He'd once again fooled the fans and diverted the paparazzi before the real Ash left his hotel for the gig at the Dallas arena. A few photographers had lingered behind, hoping for an exclusive shot of the rock star's new girlfriend. But Charley, along with Ash in a hoodie and dark glasses, had managed to evade detection, departing from a side entrance thirty minutes later. The two Ash Wilds had eventually been reunited in the venue's dressing room.

Now disguised in a baseball cap and horn-rimmed glasses, Pete stood beside Charley and Jessie, his backstage pass worn like a medal of honor on his chest. He had the biggest grin on his face as his idol entertained the Dallas crowd.

"How are you enjoying the show from backstage?" Charley asked him.

"It's amazing," he replied, his gaze not wavering from his rock-star hero. "I feel this affinity with Ash. It's like we're one."

Charley just nodded. The background check had revealed that Pete lived in Norwich, England, with his grandmother. He was actually seventeen years old, but looked and behaved much younger. He worked for a delivery company and had a high school diploma to his name, and held no criminal convictions. The boy was totally unexceptional. He simply seemed to live his life through Ash, as confirmed by the photo he'd posted on a Wildling fan site of his bedroom plastered with Ash Wild posters and memorabilia. For that reason alone, Charley thought the boy a little weird and intended to keep a close eye on him.

When the band kicked off with the track "Been There, Done That," Pete started busting moves, playing air guitar and belting out the words to the song. Charley and Jessie exchanged glances, trying not to laugh. Pete may have looked like Ash and been able to replicate his dance routine, but he certainly couldn't sing like him.

"Hey, Pete! Do you want your own mic?" suggested Jessie, grabbing a microphone from a nearby stand.

Pete glared at her, his eyes flashing like a wild animal's and his lips curling into a snarl. Any resemblance to Ash vanished, and for a moment, Charley thought he might pounce on Jessie.

Then the bearded roadie Joel intervened and snatched the mic back from her. "I told you before—*don't* touch the gear!" he hissed.

The joke having fallen flat, Jessie meekly apologized and backed away. Pete returned to staring at his idol, the mocking apparently forgotten.

Onstage Ash proved why he was such a superstar, dazzling the audience with a guitar solo that would have made Jimi Hendrix proud. In response the Dallas crowd almost lifted the roof with their screams. Charley spotted the chef from the previous evening in the front row with his two daughters. He looked to be having the time of his life.

When the song came to an end, the stage lights faded and the roadie hurried past Charley to set up the stage for Ash's final acoustic set. This was the part of the show Charley enjoyed best. Stripped of all the high-end production, video effects, dancers and backing band, this was Ash at his most pure and honest.

A boy, his guitar and a voice.

It was hard for anyone not to fall in love with him when he performed like this.

The arena darkened until a single spot illuminated Ash in a halo of golden light at the tip of the guitar-shaped stage. He adjusted his stool, checked the tuning on his acoustic guitar, then put his lips to the mic. At once, his whole body went rigid and he keeled sideways, crashing to the floor.

15

Charley raced out onto the stage. She had no idea what had happened. Had a fan thrown something at Ash? Was it a heart attack? Had he been shot? Had the maniac promising "no more encores" struck? Whatever the cause, her overriding instinct was to protect him from further harm—if he was still alive.

The whole arena had fallen into stunned and horrified silence as Ash lay motionless in a heap at the far end of the stage. For Charley, the guitar-shaped runway seemed to extend forever as she sprinted toward his inert body.

A technician reached Ash first. He took hold of Ash's shoulder, then shuddered, jerked his hand away and fell backward. In that instant Charley knew what was wrong. Ash had been shocked by the electric charge.

Picking up the fallen wooden stool, Charley shoved the lethal microphone away from Ash's body. She checked for any other dangers, then knelt down beside Ash, praying he wasn't dead. An electric shock with a strong enough current could stop the heart.

"ASH!" she called, but there was no response.

Confirming his airway was clear, she checked his breathing and circulation. His pulse was a little weak, though the fact he had a pulse was reassuring. The problem was . . . he *wasn't* breathing.

This time Charley knew Ash wasn't faking it.

Pinching his nose, she leaned over him, covered his mouth with her lips and began CPR. She was vaguely aware of anxious tour crew and security gathering around her. The offending microphone was isolated and disconnected. A stretcher was brought down by two medics. The audience were softly whispering and weeping as they watched the scene play out. Still Charley kept up her rescue breaths, focusing on the task at hand and not letting panic control her emotions.

"Charley, it's Big T," said a voice in her ear. "The medics can take over."

Charley shook her head and persisted with CPR. Ash was her responsibility. She would not let him die in her arms.

"You *need* to let them do their job," insisted Big T.

Feeling a gentle hand on her shoulder, Charley nodded and finished her set of rescue breaths. She was on her last one when all of a sudden Ash regained consciousness. His eyes flickered open, and he took several breaths on his own.

"Hey, Charley . . ." he said, smiling. "Hope you're not going to break my arm for this."

"No," she replied with a relieved smile, recalling her previous threat about if he ever tried kissing her again. "As you said, it's worth the risk."

One of the medics helped Ash sit up. Seeing their idol rise from the dead, the whole audience applauded and whooped.

"Okay, let's get you to the hospital," said the medic.

"Later," said Ash, waving off his help. "I have a gig to finish."

"But we need to do a thorough medical examination," insisted the medic.

"I feel fine," declared Ash, standing up on his own. "If Dave Grohl can finish a Foo Fighters tour with a broken leg, I can certainly perform after a little shock to the system."

"Little?" queried the medic. "You were knocked unconscious and stopped breathing."

"That's rock 'n' roll for you!" Ash laughed. "Besides, can't you hear that?"

His legion of fans stamped their feet and chanted, "ASH! ASH! ASH!"

"The show must go on," he said, grabbing a wireless mic.

Charley thought Ash was a little high on adrenaline, but

otherwise he seemed unharmed. It was nothing short of a miracle. Ash took hold of Charley's hand and raised it to the sky.

"Talk about the kiss of life," he announced to loud wolf whistles and rapturous applause. "My guardian angel!"

16

Ash Wild must have the nine lives of a cat! How else could that sniveling, screeching pop prince defy death twice*? It's beyond belief. That boy deserves to die. Has to die. Must die.*

I should have shot him that first night. Why on earth didn't I pull the trigger?

I might have missed, that's why . . . Don't be stupid, you had him in your laser sight. The man at the gun store said it was just a matter of point and shoot . . . Wherever the red dot was, the bullet would go. So why didn't I pull the trigger?

Just admit it! You didn't have the guts, did you?

No.

The gun was too personal, too hands-on. And too risky. The police would easily have traced the bullets and gun. Besides, that troublesome girl interfered. Ran Ash off the stage before I could change my mind and fire. It's her fault.

That's why an accidental death is a far better idea. No one can foresee it. No one can stop it.

The spotlight took a lot of planning, though—the exact positioning of the light, the removal of the safety chain, the sabotaging of the clamp, the precise timing of the fall—every detail had to be accounted for. Then the little ego-fueled superstar lands in the wrong bloody place!

How unfair is that? Less than an inch or so between life and death.

Ash certainly had a guardian angel watching over him then.

At least the microphone was easier to tamper with. I don't know why I didn't think of that in the first place. The only tricky part was ensuring Ash would be the victim.

But the plan worked—like a dream.

Oh, the thrill! The sheer joy when Ash dropped dead!

Then that wretched girl again, the Wildcat. She brought him back to life.

It was her fault, his guardian angel. Yeah, all her *fault!*

Next time . . . I'll guarantee she can't save her precious rock star.

Next time . . . he won't rise from the ashes. Nor will she.

17

Charley closed the door to her hotel room and collapsed on the bed. It was just past midnight and she was exhausted. But she had to report in to Guardian. They'd want an update on the situation.

Her finger paused over the Dial button. She still hadn't spoken with Blake. Since she was using the official Guardian line, though, he'd have to answer her call now. Both dreading and needing to talk to him, Charley took a deep breath and dialed.

The phone rang three times before it was picked up and a voice answered. "Report in."

She hesitated. "W-where's Blake?"

"He's been reassigned," Jason explained. "I'm now your official contact."

"Oh . . ." said Charley, disappointed yet somewhat relieved that she wouldn't have to speak to Blake.

"Don't sound so pleased to hear my voice," said Jason. "I'm

equally happy to be working with you. Now, are you going to update me on your Principal or not?"

"Sorry," Charley replied, a little thrown by the change in contact. She felt awkward talking with Jason when they didn't exactly get along. "Well . . . according to the doctor, Ash is all okay. After finally being convinced to take a ten-minute break for a medical checkup, he finished the gig to a standing ovation." She half smiled at the thought, still in awe of Ash's dedication to his fans. "But he was extremely lucky to survive—that direct shock to the head could have fried his brain."

"I've seen some of the fan footage online," said Jason. "Looks like he was shot by a stun gun. Any idea what went wrong?"

"Faulty microphone," Charley replied. "The sound technician says the wiring wasn't grounded properly. Terry—the tour manager—is furious. He's got the whole tech team retesting the electrical setup before the next concert. He says these things *shouldn't* happen."

"Well, it did," said Jason. "Kay just called the colonel to praise your fast response. She credits you with saving Ash's life."

Charley felt a flush of pride.

"Kay's also reviewing all security measures with Big T," Jason went on, "so don't be surprised if there's a bit of a shake-up in the ranks. She wasn't happy with the rest of his team's response to the situation, so she's flying out to join the tour and keep a closer eye on things."

"Big T did mention Kay was concerned."

"Well, Ash does seem prone to accidents on this tour," remarked Jason.

"Accidents don't just happen," said Charley, repeating the sinister message that had popped up on Ash's computer.

"What? You think this was another attempt on Ash's life?"

"Yes."

"But isn't using a microphone to kill someone rather hit-or-miss?" Jason wondered. "Anyone could have used that mic before Ash. A roadie during the sound check or one of the band in the show."

"True. But the night before the concert, Ash showed me his social media feed. There was a whole bunch of posts from haters, but one, apparently from a fan, read, 'Hoping for an electrifying performance!' That's too much of a coincidence for me. Someone wants Ash dead, and they're going to great lengths to make it look like an accident."

Jason went quiet for a moment. "Then the question is, who is this fan?"

"Exactly. If we could trace the two online messages, and any others sent by the same accounts, then we might identify the user. I know Big T didn't get anywhere with the first message, but perhaps Bugsy has access to higher-level resources?"

"Bugsy's away on an assignment for the colonel," informed Jason, "but I'll ask that newbie, Amir, if he can help. I hear he's something of a whiz with computers."

"Thanks," said Charley, surprised at how willing Jason was to help. Perhaps it wouldn't be so hard to work with him after all. "I'll e-mail you the links now."

She pulled up Ash's social media page on her phone and searched for the two suspect messages. With a couple of taps, she forwarded them to Jason.

"Got 'em," said Jason. "Anything else before we sign off?"

Charley hesitated. "Jason . . . is Blake there?"

There was a long pause and muffled voices, one of which sounded like Blake's. Jason came back on the line. "Sorry, he's out on an errand."

Charley felt her eyes prickle with tears. It was obvious Blake was there. He just didn't want to talk to her. Stifling a sob, she went into the bathroom and grabbed a tissue from the box next to the sink.

"Hey," said Jason, his voice lowered. "Forget about Blake, Charley. You're better off without him. You need to focus on the mission. Besides, you're the girlfriend of a famous rock star now!" He went on. "Not a bad swap for you. I mean, how much better could it get?"

Dabbing at her eyes, Charley looked up from the basin and let out a small cry.

"You all right?" he asked.

"Yeah, everything's fine," replied Charley in a voice as calm as she could manage. She hadn't cried out because of Blake. On the bathroom mirror, scrawled in her own red lipstick, were the words

TO BE AN ANGEL
U NEED 2 DIE FIRST!

18

"If you're my girlfriend, you should really be holding my hand," said Ash as the two of them arrived in a stretch limo outside the Bellagio Hotel in Las Vegas.

Since Dallas, the tour had taken them to Kansas City, then through Minneapolis and Denver to the entertainment capital of the world. With a day off between gigs, his manager had acquired VIP invites for Ash to attend an exclusive star-studded fashion show before his concert the next night at the Mandalay Bay Events Center—and it would be Ash and Charley's first official appearance as a couple.

Ash offered his hand. He seemed totally at ease with the arrangement made by his manager and Colonel Black—in fact he looked proud to have her on his arm. Considering Ash could date almost any girl on the planet, Charley felt flattered by this. She took his hand, telling herself it was purely to keep up appearances. But after the messy breakup with Blake and the deluge of hate messages online, she couldn't deny it was a much-needed boost to her battered self-esteem.

He smiled, gave her hand a reassuring squeeze, then stepped out into a blaze of camera flashes.

The press were out in full force. The fashion show was a focal point for all the celebrities in Las Vegas, and a long red carpet had been laid for their arrival. An event coordinator had requested that Ash stop halfway along the red carpet for his official photo op. Dressed in a black silk shirt, jacket and coal-black designer jeans, he looked the epitome of the teen rock star. Charley, in a sleek satin gown and high heels that Ash's stylist had picked out for her, caught everyone's eye, more than fulfilling her role as the chic, glamorous girlfriend. The cameras simply couldn't get enough of the cool young couple.

As they posed for photos, Charley kept her designer sunglasses on. She couldn't risk getting dazzled by all the flashes. She may have become Ash's "girlfriend," but she was still his bodyguard. Her eyes scanned the huddle of photographers and, to her dismay, spotted Gonzo's rat-face among the pack. How on earth had the lowlife gotten an official press pass?

Still smiling for the cameras, Charley surveyed the crush of tourists and fans behind the metal barriers, checking for signs of a potential threat—those directed not only at Ash but also at herself.

For she was now a target too.

That had been made abundantly clear by the sinister threat left on her bathroom mirror. After taking a picture for evidence, she'd wiped away the lipstick-smeared message and hadn't mentioned it to anyone for fear of being pulled off the assignment. If she couldn't protect herself, then how could she be considered fit to protect Ash?

As more celebrities spilled out of limos to make their way across the red carpet, Big T came up alongside and indicated they should enter the hotel. Accompanying them, he kept at a respectful but responsive distance, his massive bulk a high-profile deterrent to any troublemakers. They entered the famous Bellagio lobby, its ceiling adorned with two thousand handblown glass flowers, the display suspended over their heads like a glistening rainbow. Ushered through to the ballroom, Charley found herself among a menagerie of movie stars, musicians, TV personalities and supermodels—many of them drawn to Ash and eager to meet his new girlfriend.

"Hey, Ash, how ya doing?" drawled an impossibly handsome and instantly recognizable figure.

"Hi, Kyle, good to see you again," said Ash, embracing the movie star like an old friend.

"And this must be Charley, your guardian angel." Kyle lifted the back of her hand to his lips. "*Definitely* an angel."

For a moment Charley was speechless. Luckily a bow-tied

waiter approached and offered her a glass of sparkling water, giving her a chance to compose herself. "Thank you . . . I'm sure everyone says this, but I love your films. No one does action movies like you."

"Hey, I only act the hero," he said humbly. "You're the *real* action hero." He did a couple of karate punches. "I saw those photos from Miami. You were like Bruce Lee with that palm strike! Ash, I'm surprised you even need Big T anymore," he said, glancing at the bald-headed veteran behind them. "You should just hire Charley to be your bodyguard."

Ash laughed. "It had crossed my mind."

Charley gave a small smile, but Big T's jaw clenched and he clearly didn't appreciate the joke.

They circulated among the other guests, Ash introducing Charley to more A-list celebrities than she had ever dreamed possible. The glamorous side of his superstar life was intoxicating, and she had to keep reminding herself that she wasn't there for her own enjoyment but for Ash's protection.

At last the guests were called for the start of the show. With reserved seats in the front row, she and Ash were in prime position next to the catwalk. But no place was reserved for Big T, and he was relegated to the ballroom entrance. The house lights dimmed and a thumping dance track blasted out of the speakers. Spotlights lit up the runway stage, and a long-legged model glided out from the wings. Wearing a gorgeous dress that shimmered like moonlight, she was greeted by collective gasps of delight and wonder. Another model appeared and strutted down the catwalk in an equally breathtaking design, her off-the-shoulder kimono-inspired gown seeming to have been spun from spider silk.

The ballroom was abuzz as ever more cutting-edge fashions were paraded in front of the celebrity audience. But Charley paid little attention to the clothes and the models. Her mind was too distracted. It kept returning to the ominous message on the mirror.

TO BE AN ANGEL
U NEED 2 DIE FIRST!

The key question was: who had written it?

A jealous fan? With a hurricane of abuse online for being Ash's girlfriend, that was a strong possibility. She'd have to keep tabs on any repeat haters to see if there was a link. But how had the fan accessed her locked hotel room?

This made her think it could be one of the band members. If it was, perhaps the death threat was just a tour prank? She'd witnessed the guys playing some pretty cruel jokes on one another. Everything from itching powder on the toilet seat to duct-taping their belongings to the hotel ceiling to swapping shampoo for pink hair dye.

But this message didn't feel like a joke, not with the

threats made against Ash. Could the maniac trying to kill Ash now want her dead by association? That was a distinct possibility.

Charley figured whoever had written the message wanted to frighten her. Why else give a warning first?

"I don't believe it," said Ash, his jaw dropping open in shock.

"What?" said Charley, suddenly on high alert.

"It's Hanna."

A gorgeous girl with dark brown locks who looked to be around Charley's age was parading in a showstopping bejeweled silver dress. As she approached the end of the catwalk, she spied Ash. There was a momentary flare of recognition in her eyes, and then she pirouetted away and strode back down the stage.

Ash spent the rest of the show squirming in his seat every time his ex-girlfriend appeared. The model seemed to be purposely strutting in front of him.

After the show, the guests mingled and chatted, the stunning designs a focus of most conversations. As Ash and Charley did the rounds, Hanna made her appearance. She now wore hipster jeans and a cropped white bodice-top, and her glossy hair was pulled into a tight ponytail. With only the lightest touch of makeup, her natural beauty was stunningly apparent. Charley instantly felt out of her league.

But Hanna's attitude certainly didn't match her looks. "So,

you're into blondes now? I thought it was redheads," the model said cuttingly to her ex-boyfriend.

Ash gave a pained look. "Hanna, I've said I'm sorry. Many times."

Hanna looked down her nose at Charley. "I'd be careful if I were you. You're playing with fire."

Charley responded with a civil smile. "I'm used to getting my fingers burned," she replied.

"Well, as long as you've got your eyes wide open. He's not to be trusted."

"Hey, I'm still here," said Ash, mortified by her scathing comments.

"More's the pity," said Hanna, turning on her heel and sashaying away.

Ash stared after her, a wounded look on his face.

"She doesn't like you very much, does she?" remarked Charley.

He shook his head. "I don't blame her. I made a stupid mistake. Let's go. This party's lost its appeal."

Charley followed Ash back into the lobby, Big T falling in behind. As they exited the hotel, the line of cameramen beckoned for a photo, but Ash wasn't in the mood to play the gracious rock star. He headed straight for the limo.

Then Gonzo taunted. "Hasn't Hanna forgiven you?"

Ash shot him a ferocious glare.

"I've still got the picture I took of you and that redhead," goaded Gonzo, snapping away at Ash's scowl. "That was a real money shot."

Charley saw Ash flush with anger and turn on Gonzo. Before he could launch himself at the lowlife, Charley pulled Ash back and bundled him into the limo.

19

"What about this one?" asked Ash, pointing to a solid gold Rolex in the jewelry store's display case.

"Very nice," said Charley. But she barely gave the watch a second glance. Her senses were on full alert. She was convinced someone was following them.

They were browsing in the Grand Canal Shoppes mall inside the Palazzo Hotel. A mini indoor Venice, it boasted high-end designer shops, upscale boutiques and even water-filled canals complete with gondolas to take people around the mall.

Pete had once again led the paparazzi on a wild goose chase, allowing Ash and Charley to slip away unseen. Ash had admitted he was feeling a little low, and Kay had recommended some retail therapy before his gig that evening. At first Charley had thought Ash was in a bad mood because he'd bumped into his ex-girlfriend, but then she recalled the day's date from the operation folder. It was the anniversary of his mother's death.

As Ash continued to browse the rows of designer watches, Charley studied the reflection in the plate glass of the store window. Applying her anti-surveillance training, she was looking for multiple sightings and any sign of unnatural behavior among the passing shoppers: people peeping around corners, fidgeting or acting shifty, showing a vacant expression, talking to themselves or fixated on their target.

A steady stream of tourists and shoppers ambled by. Some loitered, others browsed, a few took vacation snaps by the mock canals. There weren't any faces Charley recognized, and no individual stood out from the crowd.

Yet her gut told her someone was out there, watching, waiting, preying on them.

"Have you seen these bracelets, Charley?" said Ash, beckoning her into the adjacent store.

The shop assistant welcomed them and laid out a selection of silver and gold designs. Ash ran his gaze over them, then turned to Charley. "Which one do you like the best?" he asked.

Charley took a moment from her surveillance to have a quick glance. Her eyes were instantly drawn to a simple bracelet woven from three bands of white gold. "That one's beautiful," she said.

"I'll get it for you," said Ash, pulling out his wallet.

"But it's five thousand dollars!" protested Charley.

He smiled at her. "So? You're worth it."

Charley put her hand over his wallet. "Listen, it's very sweet of you, Ash. But I can't accept it."

Ash ignored her, handed the shop assistant his debit card and looped the white-gold bracelet around Charley's wrist. "A thank-you gift," he said. "For saving my life."

As she admired the exquisite piece of jewelry, wondering how she could refuse now, Charley heard the faintest click of a camera.

"It'll be an engagement ring next," said a snide voice.

At once she knew who'd been following them. Charley couldn't believe it. Was there no place Gonzo couldn't find them? Hounded at every turn, tormented at every moment, she was truly experiencing the claustrophobic nightmare of being a celebrity in the twenty-first century—no privacy, no boundaries, no escape.

Gonzo was their very own stalker.

"Go crawl back into whatever sewer you came from!" Ash snapped.

"That's no way to treat a friend," replied the pap.

"Friend? Even my worst enemy is more of a friend than you."

"Harsh, but you've got a lot of enemies from what I hear."

Fuming, Ash stormed out of the store.

"Just leave us alone, Gonzo," said Charley, struggling to keep the anger out of her voice.

But Gonzo stalked them through the shopping mall, snapping and filming away nonstop. Each time they entered a store, he'd wait outside, his lens tracking their every movement.

"I'll have you arrested," Charley threatened as they came out of a boutique.

"I know my rights. I'm on public property—nothing you can do about it."

Charley felt her fury rising. Even while they had lunch, the man's camera recorded their every mouthful. They visited a designer clothes store. When they came out, they passed a florist, and Gonzo goaded Ash once again. "How about a bouquet for your girlfriend? And don't forget . . . one for your mother! Lilies are a good choice."

Charley noticed Ash's eyes redden and his fists clench. Gonzo had taken it too far, even for a paparazzo. Charley felt something snap inside her too. What right did this piece of scum have to stalk and harass them? What right did he have to bring up Ash's dead mother? What right did he have to bait people purely for the purposes of a "unique" photo he could sell for thousands?

Charley reached into her bag and pulled out a small canister. Before Gonzo knew what was happening, she sprayed his camera lens and face with red gel. Spluttering and swearing, Gonzo furiously tried to wipe the gunk from his eyes.

"Sorry about that," said Charley. "It just went off in my hand by accident."

As Charley sauntered away with Ash, who was staring at her in stunned admiration, Gonzo yelled after them, "You'll live to regret that, *chica*!"

20

Charley woke to the insistent blare of her alarm clock. Surely it couldn't be morning already. Often on this tour she was so exhausted that she lost track of time, with no idea what day it was, let alone which hotel she was sleeping in. After a while the bedrooms all looked the same. She vaguely recalled they'd reached San Francisco. The gig in Las Vegas had gone without a hitch, as had the ones in Salt Lake City and Seattle, and they were now entering the final phase of the tour. She only had to keep Ash safe a few more days, and then the threat of "no more encores" would be just that—an empty threat.

Groggily, she reached over to switch off the clock. But the alarm continued to ring in her ears. Shrugging off sleep, she smelled the acrid tinge of smoke in the air. At once she sat bolt upright in bed.

FIRE!

Barefoot and wearing a T-shirt and shorts, Charley grabbed Ash's spare key card from the bedside table and sprinted for the door. Bugsy's emergency fire training had drilled into her that every second counted in a fire. She tested the temperature of the door handle, then pressed the back of her hand to the door itself. Both were cool to the touch. Confident she wouldn't stumble straight into a blaze, she opened the door and peered out.

A noxious gray haze immediately enveloped her, and she started coughing. The corridor was filled with smoke. Guests in all states of dress and undress were fleeing in panic, many with no idea where the nearest fire escapes were and running the wrong way. Jessie and Zoe flew past, along with other members of the road crew.

"Have you seen Ash?" Charley called out.

"No!" cried Zoe, not stopping as she disappeared into the haze of smoke.

Pulling her T-shirt up to her mouth, Charley hammered on Ash's door. No answer.

She guessed that Big T had already evacuated him. But she couldn't take that chance. Slotting the key card into the lock, she accessed his suite.

"ASH?" she called, hurrying through the lounge to the bedroom.

A figure lay sprawled underneath the covers. Charley

wondered how on earth Ash could sleep through the Klaxon of the fire alarm. Then she spotted his in-ear noise-cancellation headphones.

Charley shook Ash awake. "GET UP!" she shouted.

Ash blearily opened his eyes. "What! W-what's going on?"

"Fire!" explained Charley as she dashed into the bathroom and soaked a couple of hand towels. When she came back, Ash was busy gathering up his songbook, laptop and acoustic guitar. "Leave them! We don't have time."

"My life ain't worth living without my guitar," said Ash as he stuffed his songbook into his shorts.

"If we don't get out *now*, you won't have a life, never mind a guitar!" She grabbed his arm and hauled him to the door. She opened it a crack and smoke surged into the room. She slammed it shut.

Ash looked to the balcony. "Why don't we jump?" he suggested.

Charley gave a strained smile. "We could. But the pool's on the other side."

She handed him a dripping wet towel. "Put this over your mouth and stay close."

Crouching low to the floor to avoid the worst of the smoke, she eased the door open and led Ash out. The corridor was now a darkening tunnel of gray-white fog. It was impossible to see more than a few feet ahead. She could hear a few straggling guests coughing and spluttering, and in the far distance the howl of fire engines. From her security checks on arrival at the hotel, she knew the nearest fire exit was eight doors and one corridor down. Keeping a hand to the wall, she counted them off as they scurried like frightened mice along the carpet. Her eyes stung from the toxic smoke, and she now appreciated how easily a person could get disoriented in a fire. There was no sense of distance or direction; everywhere was a murky gray cloud, furniture and figures appearing and disappearing like ghosts.

After what seemed like an eternity, they reached the fire door. She pushed against the locking bar, but it wouldn't budge. Charley shoved harder. To no avail. Now she knew why the hotel guests had been fleeing in the other direction.

"Let me . . . have a go," Ash coughed, taking the damp towel from his mouth.

He kicked at the bar. Nothing. So he slammed his shoulder against the door. This time it screeched open a fraction. A lick of flames shot out. Ash leaped back, yelling as the sleeve of his shirt caught fire. The flames rapidly spread across his back.

On impulse Charley dragged him to the floor and rolled him on the carpet. At the same time, she smothered him with her body. She knew her T-shirt was fireproof and prayed she could put out the flames before Ash was seriously burned.

"I'm . . . all right," gasped Ash, his shirt singed black.

But they were now in even more immediate danger. The corridor was on fire. Despite the door being open only a crack, it was enough for the blaze on the other side to finger its way in. Cursing herself for not checking the door first, she pulled Ash to his knees and headed back the other way. They'd lost their wet towels, and their lungs now filled with suffocating smoke. Coughing and choking, they crawled along the corridor. But in their hurry to escape the advancing flames, Charley lost count of the doors. With no clue in which direction or how far the next fire exit was, the two of them stumbled on blindly.

Ash was coughing uncontrollably and Charley's head pounded and she felt sick. The flames would be the least of their worries. She knew from Bugsy that the majority of deaths in a fire were caused by smoke inhalation rather than burns. They had to escape the corridor and find clear air.

Blinking away acrid tears, Charley reached out desperately in front of her. In the gloom, she discovered that a door to a guest room had been left ajar. Pulling Ash inside, she kicked the door shut behind them. Smoke hung around the ceiling in a thick cloud and still seeped in around the frame. But it was a far better situation than the corridor. Leaving Ash hacking on the floor, she threw any towels that she could find into the bath and ran the taps. As soon as the towels were wet, she stuffed them against the edges of the door.

"Charley! Look at this!" croaked Ash, leaning out of the balcony window for fresh air.

Six floors down, a huge crowd had gathered in the darkness. Fire engines, their lights flashing and reflecting off the other buildings, jammed the streets. The beam of a searchlight swept the hotel and illuminated the two of them in the window.

Ash looked at Charley, his face streaked black with soot, and said, "Take a leap of faith?"

With a final glance back at the smoldering door, Charley nodded and climbed over the balcony. Hand in hand, they jumped.

21

"I hate to admit it," said Kay, shaking her head wearily as they ate breakfast in the diner opposite the fire-damaged hotel, "but that makes a great picture!"

She tapped the newspaper with a manicured fingernail. Below the headline—"LOVEBIRDS FLEE NEST FIRE"—was a photo of Ash and Charley caught midplunge over the hotel pool, still clasping each other's hands, the flaming building making a dramatic backdrop to their death-defying escape. Of course, Gonzo had been there to catch the moment in all its glory, along with a handful of other paparazzi in the city. But *he* had been the one to nab the front-page shot.

"The headline's predictably trashy, though," Kay went on, sipping from her coffee. Despite having been up most of the night, as had everyone else, she somehow managed to retain her elegant looks even in a hotel robe and slippers. Charley and Ash were wrapped in blankets, Big T in a white T-shirt and gray jogging pants and, much to the road crew's amusement, Terry had fled the hotel in a pair of blue pajamas embroidered with yellow teddy bears. Only Jessie had managed to escape the fire in any reasonable state of dress. She sat with Zoe at the next table in jeans, T-shirt and sneakers.

"But, in all seriousness, either this tour is cursed with the worst bad luck or someone is seriously committed to killing Ash if they're willing to burn down an entire hotel." Kay put a protective arm around her nephew and smiled at Charley. "If it wasn't for you, Charley, my Ash wouldn't be sitting here with us now having breakfast."

"Yeah, well done, Charley," said Big T, cupping a mug of coffee between his huge hands. "But next time . . . take the stairs." He forced a tired smile at his weak joke.

Kay turned to Big T. "Might I ask where *you* were during all this? Because you certainly weren't at Ash's side."

Big T dropped his grin and responded with a defensive frown. "I'm not sure what you're getting at, Ms. Gibson. When the fire alarm woke me, I discovered Ash already gone from his room. So, after ensuring everyone else was out, I made my escape. I was the *last* of the crew to leave our floor."

A frosty look entered Kay's green eyes. "Not quite the last, as it turned out. Ash was still up there!"

"With Charley," he pointed out. "I knew she'd carried out the fire security check, so I was confident she'd get Ash to safety."

"Yes, and thank God she did!" said Kay, turning her back on Big T.

Charley saw the wounded look on the old bodyguard's lined face. She wanted to say something in his defense, but Zoe cut in from the next table. "Hey, listen to this! Latest update on CNN . . . The fire was no accident!" she exclaimed, reading from a news app on her smartphone. "The police report states it was arson . . . They've found what appears to be the remnants of a homemade incendiary bomb." She showed them a picture of a charred can of Hurtle energy drink and the remains of a cheap digital watch. "The fire was started in a housekeeping storage cupboard . . . and someone had disabled the hotel's sprinkler system!"

Big T leaned forward in his seat. "Any suspects?"

Zoe read a little farther down, then shook her head. "The police have no leads whatsoever . . . and no one has claimed responsibility so far."

Charley put down her orange juice. "The fire *had* to be targeted at Ash."

Ash glanced up from his omelet, his fork hanging halfway between the plate and his open mouth.

"Fire is a very indiscriminate method of murder," Big T noted. "Ash may have escaped unharmed, but other guests didn't. It's a miracle so few were actually hurt in the blaze."

"But if some maniac is willing to go to those lengths," Charley pointed out, "it shows how determined they are."

Kay narrowed her eyes. "Aside from the death threats we know about, what makes you think Ash was targeted?"

"Our closest fire exit was blocked," Charley explained.

Zoe gasped and looked at Jessie. "Thank heaven you made me run the other way."

Jessie nodded. "Yeah, we'd have been trapped too!"

"Good thing you did," said Ash, setting down his fork. "The fire was on the other side of the door. Without Charley smothering me, I'd have been burned to a crisp."

He took Charley's hand in his. She smiled warmly in response. Their near-death experience had definitely brought them closer.

Big T rubbed his chin thoughtfully. "It might not have been blocked on purpose. Many fire doors have smoke seals that expand under heat to close the gap between the door and its frame. The fact they worked in this case probably saved your lives."

"That does seem more likely than a direct attack on Ash," admitted Kay.

The diner's entrance swung open, and Vince approached their table. "I've been informed that it's safe to return to the hotel and collect our belongings," said their security guard.

"Well, thank God for the San Francisco fire department," said Kay. "I just hope they managed to save my dresses." She raised an eyebrow in response to Terry's shocked expression. "That's a joke, Terry, in case you're wondering."

They rose from the table and headed back to the hotel. From the outside there appeared to be little damage, just a few shattered windows and black smears of soot staining the outer walls. As they entered the lobby, the reception area was in organized chaos, but a VIP representative from the hotel swiftly escorted their group past security and up the stairs.

The benefits of being a celebrity, thought Charley.

On the sixth floor, she and the others were confronted by the full devastation wreaked by the blaze. The corridor was scorched and the walls were blackened. The harsh, acrid tang of smoke still hung in the air, and the carpet was soaked with water from the fire hoses. As they each peeled off to gather their belongings, Charley was amazed to discover her and Ash's rooms were untouched by the fire, their closed doors having held back the flames. There was still the reek of smoke, but that appeared to be the only serious damage.

Next door she heard Ash exclaim his delight at finding his guitar in one piece. She looked in and smiled to herself when she saw him caressing the instrument like a long-lost lover. But she noticed the Intruder device that she'd attached to Ash's door frame had melted beyond repair.

Returning to her room, Charley checked and repacked the contents of her go-bag: spare Intruders, half-empty pepper spray, high-impact pen, first-aid kit, comms unit, flashlight.

As expected, her phone registered several missed calls from Guardian HQ—Jason's concern growing with each voice mail message—and a bunch of warning texts from the Intruder device catching her entering and leaving Ash's room during the fire. She deleted these, then called HQ.

The phone was picked up on the first ring. "Charley! Is Ash okay?" asked Jason.

"Yes, he's fine," she replied. "I am too. Thanks for asking."

"That's a relief," he said, though Charley wasn't sure if he was referring to her or Ash or both of them. "We saw the fire on the news and pictures of your dramatic escape, but we were worried that we hadn't heard from you."

"I'd left my phone in the room. For obvious reasons, I was in a bit of a rush to get out," she explained. "But I've got your messages now."

"Yeah, the colonel insisted that I keep calling."

"And I was beginning to think you cared."

"Not a chance," Jason replied. "Report in later." Then, before signing off, he added, "Stay safe, Charley."

"Will do," she replied, unable to suppress a smile at his note of concern.

Putting the phone back in her bag, she hunted through her suitcase for some clean clothes that didn't stink too much of smoke. She was now grateful for Bugsy's foresight in supplying fireproof clothing. As she pulled on a pair of jeans, she noticed a white hotel envelope on the carpet behind the door. She picked it up, frowned at the blank front and peeled open the seal. Inside was a clipping from a tabloid magazine: Gonzo's photo of her with Ash at the restaurant in Dallas. Pasted beneath it in letters cut out from a newspaper were the words

ASHES 2 ASHES, dusT 2 duST
So wILL u BE

22

Ash was certainly a trouper. Despite a sore throat from smoke inhalation and another failed attempt on his life, he was resolved to perform for his San Francisco fans at the Oakland Oracle Arena that night. He burst onto the stage with a kamikaze-like energy, his gravelly voice more than suiting his style of rock music. As Charley watched him literally rip one of his guitars apart during a solo, then set it on fire, she wondered if Ash's third brush with death had tipped him over the edge. He was acting as if this might be his last ever concert on earth.

Then again, she thought, his extreme performance might be his way of letting off steam. Whatever, this gig was jaw-dropping, and his fans, sensing Ash's desperation, were going wild for him.

Behind the scenes, Kay had taken up the reins alongside Terry as tour manager, her presence an iron rod to the band and crew alike. Nothing was being overlooked in terms of stage management or venue security. Everything had been triple-checked. The gigs were being run like a military operation.

But Charley knew someone had slipped the net.

The newspaper threat she'd received couldn't be clearer. The fire had been a premeditated attack on her and Ash. And if she needed any more proof, she'd subsequently read in a news report that the arson investigators had found the burned-out remains of a housekeeper's cart wedged behind the fire door on their floor of the hotel.

Charley had harbored a tiny hope that the message on the mirror had been a prank, a hoax or at the most a knee-jerk reaction by a jealous fan at the Dallas concert. But she could no longer delude herself.

The homicidal maniac was on the tour with them.

How else could that person know the hotels they were staying at, discover which rooms she and Ash were in and pass unquestioned through their security checks?

In order to carry out the crimes, the culprit had to have access backstage, to the hotels and to the tour bus. Only somebody with an official pass could move unseen and undetected. The idea of it chilled her blood and made her more paranoid than ever.

The enemy was definitely within!

Charley had her suspicions who the perpetrator might be, but no direct proof. The envelope with its newspaper clipping was now in the pocket of her jeans. She hadn't yet told Big T or Guardian about it. She knew that Colonel Black would instantly pull her off the assignment, and she didn't trust anyone else, not even Big T, to keep Ash safe. She had to see this assignment through to the end. It was her duty.

Besides, if the maniac was who she thought it was, then she could handle them easily enough when they showed their hand. But when would that be? And would she be in the right place at the right time to stop them?

Any mistake, delay or miscalculation in her reactions could result in Ash's death.

Charley remembered the tattoo on Big T's inner forearm. A pair of weighted scales and the words *Guilty until proven innocent*.

She couldn't afford to wait. She couldn't risk Ash's life any longer.

Pete was standing beside Jessie, bobbing and weaving in time to the music, mouthing the words in sync with Ash, as he did every night. Jessie was gazing in reverential awe at her hero on the stage, her hands clasped to her chest in deep devotion. Both had an unnatural obsession with Ash, but only one had a motive to kill him.

Convinced who it was, Charley made up her mind to act. She radioed for backup, then confronted Ash's stalker.

23

"What's all this about?" demanded Jessie as she was shoved into a chair in an empty dressing room.

Vince stood by the door, while Rick kept a hand on Jessie's shoulder and ensured she stayed seated.

"Don't play innocent with me," said Charley. "You know exactly why you're here."

Jessie's eyes flicked from Vince's impassive face to Rick's stony expression and back to the furious glare Charley was giving her. The startled girl looked like she might burst into tears at any moment. Charley thought Jessie was putting on a convincing act. But of course she'd have to be a good actress in order to con her way into everyone's trust.

"Charley, what have I done?" she pleaded.

"Aside from set fire to the hotel? Try to kill Ash."

"What?" exclaimed Jessie. "Why would I want to hurt Ash? I love him."

"That's exactly why. That's your motive. You're obsessed with Ash to the point of madness."

"No, *this* is madness. I haven't done anything but support him!" said Jessie angrily. She tried to rise, but Rick firmly pushed her back down.

The door to the dressing room opened, and Big T stormed in. "What's going on?" he demanded.

"This is who's behind all the threats and attacks on Ash," said Charley, stepping aside.

Big T stared at the frightened girl in the chair. "What, Jessie?" he said, his thick brow creasing in skepticism. "But she runs Ash's US fan club. She's his biggest fan."

"Gives her the perfect cover," argued Charley. "In order to stage these so-called accidents, she needed to have complete access to all locations. Her tour pass is the ticket to her crimes."

"You're insane!" spat Jessie. "You're making accusations without any shred of proof!"

Big T cocked his head at Charley. "She's got a point. Where's your evidence?"

"Well . . . there isn't anything that directly incriminates her," admitted Charley, "but there's a lot of circumstantial evidence that points to Jessie."

"Go on," said Big T, leaning against the wall and crossing his arms.

Charley took a deep breath. She'd been thinking hard since the discovery of the envelope that morning. "I can't say whether any of this links back to the original letter bomb or the 'no more encores' death threat. But I do know that I found Jessie sneaking around backstage the night of the spotlight accident. She was hiding behind the drum riser, right next to one of the wire-rope ladders that led up to the lighting rig."

Jessie rolled her eyes. "I told you at the time I wanted to see the stage setting like Ash does."

"I believe she'd just come down the ladder after rigging the spotlight and was checking that it was aligned with the toaster lift," Charley continued, ignoring the girl's incredulous laugh. "Next, a little before Ash was shocked, Jessie took his microphone for the acoustic set. I think she may have switched it for the faulty one."

Jessie snorted in disbelief. "Oh, come on! Really? You were there with me. How was I supposed to do that? I'm not a magician."

"But you were the only one to handle it, apart from the crew. Joel also complained that you had touched the gear before. That in itself is suspicious," responded Charley. "Then there's the fire last night. A few things have struck me as odd. First, it's funny how you knew not to go to the closest fire exit, the one that was blocked."

"I didn't know *which* way I was running," argued Jessie. "I don't think anyone did. It was chaos."

"But at breakfast Zoe said you made her run your way. Why?"

"I—I . . . don't know. I thought that way was the closest exit."

"But you just said you didn't know which way you were running. You're lying!"

Jessie began to cry, her mascara running down her plump cheeks in black lines.

Charley wasn't going to let herself be swayed by crocodile tears. "Second, I found it strange that you were fully dressed in the middle of the night. That indicates you were ready for the fire."

"I—I don't go to bed until late," sobbed Jessie. "I was updating Ash's fan website . . . Honest . . . You can look at my posts. You'll see the times I uploaded them."

"Posts can be scheduled in advance."

"Oh, you have an answer for everything, don't you?" snapped Jessie, glaring at Charley through tear-filled eyes. "You just want to get rid of me. You're the one who's paranoid. You've got your claws into Ash, and now you want to make sure no one else has him."

Charley laughed. "That's exactly what *you're* trying to do. You've admitted you love him many times. You even said that you'd kill to be in my position. You're jealous. And because you can't have him, you've decided no one will."

Leaping up from her chair, Jessie swiped her false red nails at Charley's face. "You liar!"

Charley barely managed to evade the razor-sharp points. Instinctively defending herself, she aimed a knife-hand strike to the girl's neck.

"Enough!" barked Big T, grabbing hold of her wrist. Rick seized Jessie in his arms and pulled the two girls apart. "Charley, this is all very thin. Pure speculation. Don't you have any firm proof?"

Charley took out her phone. "The day after Ash and I were photographed in the restaurant, I too started receiving death threats. Most were online, but this one was written on my bathroom mirror."

Charley brought up the photo she'd taken of the lipstick threat:

TO BE AN ANGEL
U NEED 2 DIE FIRST!

"Recognize your handwriting, Jessie?" she asked, tilting the screen in her direction. Jessie's eyes widened, and she shook her head vigorously in denial.

"Why the hell didn't you bring this to my attention sooner?" said Big T, his jaw tensing.

"I thought it was a tour prank," Charley replied. "But then I got this."

She pulled out the newspaper clipping and showed it to him.

ASHES 2 ASHES, dusT 2 duST
So wILL u BE

"I'm sure this'll be familiar to you too, Jessie," said Charley.

Jessie stared at the picture in horror. "I didn't do that," she replied, her voice small and quiet.

Big T grabbed the clipping from Charley's hand. "This is no tour prank! When did you get this?"

"I—I only just came across it . . . earlier this morning," explained Charley, stumbling over her words.

"This morning!" Big T threw his hands up in disbelief, then waved the clipping in her face. "This changes everything. This confirms the fire was a direct attack on Ash! The police need to be told. If I'd known you were under threat too, I'd—"

Charley's phone rang. She turned away from Big T and answered it. "Hello?"

The voice on the other end of the line declared, "I've done it."

24

"Done what?" asked Charley, pressing her phone to her ear.

"I've traced the accident messages—"

"Who are you speaking to?" demanded Big T.

"Amir," Charley quickly replied under her breath. "He's a wiz at IT at Guardian."

"I'm sorry it took me so long, but you didn't give me much to go on—" The excitement in the new recruit's voice was matched only by the speed at which he tried to explain his findings. "A couple of Internet posts with different accounts! But I managed to hack into them both easily enough and dig up more messages. Of course, they were dummy accounts, created with false e-mail addresses that led to fake personal information. Pretty much a dead end for your average hacker. But I reverse-tracked *how* the messages were posted."

He paused, clearly expecting Charley to be impressed at this flash of hacking insight.

"Okay . . . and?" prompted Charley, holding up a hand to keep Big T from interrupting the call.

"All of them were posted using the *same* phone," he revealed. "Obviously, the IP addresses were dynamic, so I couldn't discover it that way. And the suspect kept changing the SIM card so the phone number wasn't fixed or traceable. They're being very careful to cover their tracks. But the IMEI number of the phone itself is constant."

"IMEI number?" asked Charley, bewildered by Amir's technical lingo.

"IMEI stands for International Mobile Equipment Identity number. You can easily find out your own phone's IMEI by typing *#06# into your keypad. The number is used to identify any device that uses terrestrial cellular networks. By that, I mean nonsatellite communication. Each number is unique to its device and coded into the hardware, making it virtually impossible to change."

"That's all very informative, Amir, but how does any of that help me?"

"It means the device can be tracked!" said Amir, a broad smile evident in the tone of his voice.

Charley smiled too. She eyed Jessie. She had her now!

"Since the suspect is using prepaid SIM cards, we obviously don't know who the phone belongs to," continued Amir. "But I managed to hack the network carrier and source the current cell phone number associated with our suspect's IMEI number. I'm texting you both of them now."

Charley's phone beeped with a received message.

"I'm also updating your phone remotely with a tracker device," Amir explained. "It's a program I've designed. It'll take a minute or so to upload, but then you'll be able to pinpoint the suspect's phone to within ten feet—"

"Charley!" cut in Big T, his wrinkled face hard and unforgiving as granite. "We need to talk about this threat *now*. And I think we can let Jessie go, don't you? There's nothing credible linking her to the accidents, apart from your rather tenuous speculation."

"Guilty until proven innocent," Charley reminded him, pointing to the tattoo on his arm. She waved her phone in the air. "I've got the proof we need right here."

Turning to Jessie, she ordered, "Give me your phone."

"Why?"

"Just do it." Charley snatched the cell phone from Jessie's hand and typed in *#06# to reveal its unique IMEI number. She compared it with the one on her screen, confident of exactly what she'd find.

It didn't match.

Charley checked it again and an awful, sick feeling weighed heavily in the pit of her stomach.

Wishing the ground would swallow her up, she handed back Jessie's phone. "I'm sorry . . . I've made a mistake."

"You most certainly have!" snapped Jessie, her eyes

shooting daggers at Charley as she stomped out of the dressing room.

Big T let out a heavy sigh and shook his head in disappointment. "Charley, we have some serious talking to do."

In her despondent daze, Charley heard Amir's voice drifting up from her phone. "Hey, Charley, are you still there? The tracker app should be working now. The green dot is you. The red dot is your suspect."

Charley studied the screen. A map of the venue was displayed. The app correctly located her in the dressing room.

A red dot appeared right next to the stage.

25

How could she have been so stupid! Of course Jessie *wasn't* Ash's stalker. Barging past Big T, Charley ran for the door.

"Where are you going?" shouted Big T.

"It's Pete!" Charley cried, dodging Vince's attempt to grab her and sprinting down the corridor.

To her horror, Charley realized the killer had been left all alone and unguarded. She wasn't there. Nor were Vince, Rick or Big T. Ash was completely vulnerable to an attack . . . and she was responsible.

Shouldering a roadie aside, she rounded a corner at speed and dashed down the hallway that led to the stage. The sound of twenty thousand fans screaming echoed off the walls. Her heart was pounding in her chest almost as loud as the heavy bass thud blasting from the venue's speakers.

She'd always suspected Pete. Why hadn't she listened to her gut instincts? Yes, Jessie was the obvious and logical candidate for the infatuated stalker. But Pete was the deluded and dangerous one. His copycat behavior was a clear sign of his mental instability. What sane person would imitate their idol to the point of changing their appearance entirely and getting the exact same tattoo on their arm?

It only struck Charley now that her death threats had started right after Pete had joined the tour in his semiofficial capacity as a decoy. With his ability to pass as Ash, he could have easily accessed her room without question from security, especially since she and Ash were perceived to be a couple. Similarly, Pete had the golden opportunity to wander around backstage without anyone so much as batting an eyelash. He was Ash the rock star! He could go anywhere he wanted. Not only could he have swapped the mics, but Pete was likely the one who'd started the fire at the hotel.

And at any moment Pete could strike again.

Charley ran up the steps to the wings of the stage. In the dimly lit recesses, a couple of sound technicians were prepping gear and a small group of VIP guests huddled to one side watching the show. But where was Pete?

Charley hunted around for him. He was nowhere to be found. Perhaps he'd moved over to the opposite wing? She checked Amir's tracker app. Her green dot was now situated beside the stage; the red dot was *on* the stage.

She was too late!

Elbowing her way through a knot of VIPs, she ran onto the main stage. The music was thunderous. The spotlights were blinding and she had to shield her eyes as she looked for Pete. Was he among the dancers? The band? The front row? Or already attacking Ash?

The dancers were moving at such a frenetic pace it was hard to keep track of everyone. Ash was strutting down the stage's guitar neck, singing for all he was worth to the audience, lost in the zone. But Pete wasn't anywhere to be seen. She rechecked the tracker app. The red dot definitely located him on the stage, less than fifty feet from where she stood. Maybe Amir's app didn't work after all.

"Get off the stage!" hissed a beer-bellied roadie, yanking Charley by the arm.

As she was dragged back into the wings, she happened to glance up and notice the lighting rig. Of course, the app only displayed a two-dimensional map. Pete could be right above her. Squinting, she searched the rig. It was difficult to make out much against the multiple banks of flashing lights, but she could see the spotlight operators in their suspended chairs, tracking Ash with their focus beams. If Pete was up there, they'd surely know about it and would have radioed security by now. All the wire-rope ladders had been hauled up before the start of the concert, so how would Pete have climbed there midshow?

The song "Every Day Like the Sun" came to an end, and the drummer began pounding out a distinctive backbeat. The crowd went into a frenzy as Ash launched into his

"Indestructible" routine. Above the noise, Charley heard Big T's furious voice in her earpiece.

"Charley! What's going on? Where are you? Report in right now!"

Charley couldn't think straight with all his shouting in her ear. She tugged out the wireless earpiece, pocketed it and studied the tracker app again. She racked her brains as to where Pete could be hiding. If he wasn't on the stage . . . or above it . . . he had to be *under* it!

Bounding down the steps two at a time, she reached the bottom, then dashed around to the walkway that led beneath the stage to the toaster lift. The passage was poorly lit by a scant run of bulbs, the crisscross of scaffolding to either side looking like a steel forest in a horror movie. It wasn't the sort of place to explore alone. Nevertheless she entered the passage and crept along, her eyes darting from side to side. From above, the muffled beat of "Indestructible" thumped away, sending vibrations down the steel struts.

Her face lit by the soft glow of her phone screen, she advanced deeper under the stage, watching her green dot slowly converge with the red one. Up ahead in the gloom, she spied someone moving. A figure was hunched over the hydraulic controls to the lift. He had a wrench and was uncoupling a pressure valve. Charley allowed herself a triumphant smile. She'd caught Pete in the act of sabotaging the toaster lift. She had all the proof she needed.

"Stop *right now*!" she warned, coming up behind him.

The figure spun around in shock and Charley was confronted by the roadie with the caveman-like beard. "You're not Pete," she gasped.

"No, I'm not," grunted Joel. "What are you doing under here? It's restricted access."

"What are *you* doing?" she replied, eyeing the open hydraulic unit.

He held up the wrench. "Safety inspection of the lift. We have to triple-check everything now. It's a flipping nightmare," he grumbled.

"Sorry, I was looking for someone else," she said, turning and heading back the way she'd come. Charley glanced again at her phone. On the screen her green dot sat almost right on top of the red. She peered into the dark recesses beneath the stage. Pete had to be hiding somewhere in the shadows.

Somehow she had to flush him out.

Bringing up Amir's text, she selected the number linked to the IMEI and pressed Call. In the darkness, a phone buzzed and a screen lit up.

26

If Charley hadn't turned toward the sound of the vibrating phone, her brains would have been splattered all over the floor. But she caught sight of the wrench a millisecond before it struck, and managed to dodge the fatal blow. The heavy metal tool glanced off her shoulder, sending a rivet of pain through her arm.

Crying out, she dropped her phone and staggered backward.

Joel swung the wrench again. Charley ducked and the tool clanged loudly against a metal strut. She tried to defend herself, but her arm was dead. The wrench came down and Charley dived between the scaffolding. She landed hard against a crossbeam, all the breath knocked out of her.

The roadie stepped through the gap as she tried to crawl away.

"Where you going, Wildcat?" he taunted. *"Ashes to ashes, dust to dust, so shall you be!"*

Charley's eyes widened in horror. The roadie had made the death threats! He was behind everything: the letter bomb, the spotlight, the mic, the fire . . .

The killer roadie raised the wrench above his head, a maniacal grin cutting through his thick bush of a beard like a sliver of bone. "Time for Ash's guardian angel to become a real angel!"

Charley held up her hands in a vain attempt to protect herself as Joel brought down his wrench with the force of a sledgehammer. But an overhead strut stopped the tool dead. He glanced up in stunned annoyance. Seizing her chance, Charley kicked out hard and connected with the roadie's kneecap. Joel bellowed in agony and crumpled to the floor.

Charley scrambled to her feet. As she tried to get away, he made a wild swing with the wrench and struck her across the shins. Screaming from the bone-numbing pain, she fell forward and caught her chin on a steel strut. Stars burst before her eyes. Through the ringing in her ears, Charley could still hear Ash singing, oblivious to her plight just a few feet beneath him, the music onstage drowning out the noise of their brutal fight below.

Joel began pulling himself upright. "For that I'm going to break every bone in your body, Wildcat. Ash won't even recognize you when I'm finished!"

Dazed and hurting, Charley dragged herself through the maze of scaffolding. She needed help. Glancing around, she spotted her smartphone on the floor. The roadie limped after her. Charley scrambled forward and snatched up her phone. Flicking the volume button, she turned to face her attacker.

Joel laughed. "Too late to call for help," he said, winding up to beat her senseless.

Before he could whip the wrench around, Charley darted forward and thrust the arcing stun phone into the roadie's chest. Joel's whole body convulsed, and he let out a guttural shriek. His muscles locked up, and the wrench clattered to the floor. Totally incapacitated, he toppled backward and would have fallen if not for the scaffolding behind him. Instead he hung like a limp rag doll from the bars.

"How's that for a stunning performance?" said Charley, her head still reeling from chinning the steel strut.

She leaned against the toaster lift for support. Her shins were on fire, her ribs ached, her shoulder throbbed and she tasted blood in her mouth from a split lip. Yet she knew she was lucky to be alive.

She also knew she needed backup. Charley fumbled in her pocket for her wireless earpiece.

But the iStun hadn't stayed in contact long enough to knock the roadie completely out. All of a sudden he lunged at her. Charley tried to stun him again, but he batted her arm aside and the phone went flying. Joel threw himself on top of her, and his heavy bulk sent them both crashing to the ground. In their struggle, his hands found her neck.

Charley gasped for air as he began to squeeze mercilessly.

With only seconds on her side, Charley drove the tips of her fingers into the notch above his collarbone. Joel gagged and jerked away. Charley tried to kick him off, but he was too big and strong.

Fight smarter, not harder, Jody had said.

Charley now targeted a knife-hand strike at his neck. Though she couldn't put her full force behind it, the single sharp blow to the man's jugular vein caused an involuntary muscle spasm and a burst of intense pain. Eyes bulging, he rolled away in agonized shock.

Charley found her feet. But the roadie, recovering fast, had the wrench in his hand again. As he swung wildly at her, she tried to block his attack, but her arm was still dead and her reaction too slow. The wrench hit her in the stomach. She doubled over in agony. Taking full advantage of her weakened state, Joel shoved her against the toaster lift and forced the edge of the wrench against her throat. Charley choked as she felt her windpipe being crushed.

"Where's *your* guardian angel when you need one, Wildcat?" he hissed, digging the wrench harder into her throat.

27

Charley couldn't breathe. Her feet barely touched the ground as the roadie pinned her to the side of the lift. She clawed at his face in an attempt to blind him, but her efforts to stop him from killing her were becoming weaker with every second. Her eyes rolled in their sockets, and what little light there was below the stage began to fade from her vision. Her own frantic heartbeat pounded louder in her ears than the muffled thud of the bass drum above. In the swirl of sound and fury, she'd heard the roadie hiss, *"Where's* your *guardian angel when you need one, Wildcat?"*

His savage face leered at her like a bearded devil, the bloodlust in his eyes horrifying. Then out of the darkness another face appeared, ghost-white and hairless.

"Right behind you," said the angel, swinging a massive right hook into the man's jaw that almost knocked his head clean off.

The pressure on her throat instantly ceased, and Charley

dropped to the floor. Spluttering and gasping for air, she looked up into the wrinkled face of her guardian angel.

"The legend strikes again!" Big T grinned, flexing the enormous biceps of his right arm and enlarging the words **DANGER: WEAPON OF MASS DESTRUCTION** inside his cruise-missile tattoo. "You okay?" he asked.

Rubbing at her tender throat, Charley nodded. She found it painful to swallow; otherwise she was in one piece. She glanced at the roadie now lying out cold on the floor. "Is he dead?" she croaked.

"He deserves to be," said Big T, kneeling down to check. "But he's not. So what's Joel's grudge with you? I thought you were looking for Pete."

"I was," rasped Charley. "But Joel's the one responsible for all the attacks on Ash."

Big T raised a dubious eyebrow. "Are you *certain* this time?"

Charley nodded and pointed to the hydraulic unit. "I caught him sabotaging the toaster lift. Amir's tracking app brought me to this exact location. If you look at the roadie's phone, I guarantee you'll find the IMEI number matches the phone used to post the accident messages. And I think the fact he tried to kill me confirms it all!"

"Good enough for me," said Big T. "Vince! Rick! Pick up the garbage, will you?"

Big T helped Charley to her feet. "You look like you've gone ten rounds with Mike Tyson."

"I feel it too," Charley told him, limping over to retrieve her phone.

"You're lucky Jessie spotted you going beneath the stage. I never would've found you otherwise," said Big T as he picked up the roadie's phone from the hydraulic unit. "Next time respond to my calls."

"Sorry," said Charley with a weak smile. "My earpiece fell out."

Big T narrowed his eyes, but let the matter drop.

Above, the concert was still going on, the audience screaming in delight. Charley followed Big T out from under the stage, wincing at every step. The unconscious Joel was dragged to an empty dressing room by Vince and Rick, and dumped in a chair.

Big T chucked a glass of water in the man's face. "Let's see what this scumbag has to say for himself."

Joel groaned. His eyes flickered open and darted nervously between the faces of the bodyguards. "Wha'sss . . . what's going on?" he slurred, holding his fractured jaw.

Big T bent down to eye level with the roadie. "You're being held under suspicion of attempted murder of both Ash Wild and Charley here."

"I don't know what you're talking about. I was just doing

my job, and this wildcat jumped me." He pointed an accusing finger at Charley.

Before Charley could protest, the door opened and Terry strode in. He stared at the broken-jawed roadie. "What happened to Joel?"

"He had a run-in with my fist," explained Big T. "You see, Joel's the maniac trying to kill Ash."

"Joel?" exclaimed Terry. "But he's been with the tour from the start. One of the hardest-working roadies—first to arrive and last to leave."

"Charley caught him sabotaging the toaster lift," Big T told him. "We suspect he was trying to rig another accident."

"That's not true!" Joel turned to Terry with pleading eyes. "I was following your instructions. You asked for everything to be triple-checked."

Terry nodded. "That's right, I did."

Big T held up the roadie's phone. "Charley has hard proof your phone was used to post the accident death threats against Ash."

"That's not my phone," said Joel.

Charley gasped. "That phone was right next to him. He's lying!"

Big T frowned and Charley saw his belief in her claims beginning to waver. "So why were you trying to kill Charley, then?" he demanded.

Joel put on a wounded look. "What? *She* attacked me! I was trying to restrain her."

"That's a lie too!" cried Charley. "He repeated the 'ashes to ashes' threat, then attacked me with a wrench! He's a maniac. He wants to kill Ash *and* me. Big T, you *saw* him choking me!"

Terry held up a hand. "Enough! Big T, I told you to keep this girl on a leash. First it was the laser, then the backpack bomb and now this. Attacking one of my own road crew! She's gone too far this time. I want her out and off this tour right now!"

"But—"

"No buts, Big T. You're already on thin ice with Kay. Don't give me an excuse to have you fired too!" Terry put his arm around Joel and helped him to his feet.

"Thank you, Terry," slurred Joel. "If she goes, I might not press charges."

"That's more than they deserve," said Terry, leading the injured man toward the door.

Charley watched, speechless, as the killer roadie walked free.

28

Charley knew if Joel stepped out of that door, they'd never see him again and Ash would forever be in danger.

So would she.

As the roadie limped past, the malice in his steel-blue eyes was terrifying. Compelled to act, Charley ran to block the doorway but stopped as Kay marched into the room.

"What's this about Ash's attacker being caught?" she demanded.

"Afraid not, Kay," said Terry, still supporting Joel, who had his head bowed and a hand to his fractured jaw. "It's yet another false alarm from your pet bodyguard."

Kay glanced at Charley, raising an eyebrow at her split lip and bruised throat. She turned to Big T. "What's going on here? And what happened to Charley?"

Big T glared at the roadie in Terry's arms. "I just managed to stop that man strangling Charley with a wrench."

"My God!" gasped Kay. "Why would he do that?"

"Charley didn't realize he was carrying out a safety inspection of the toaster lift," explained Big T. "It seems a case of mistaken identity. Things got out of hand and—"

"NO!" shouted Charley. "That man was sabotaging the lift to kill Ash. Why won't anyone believe me?"

Big T laid a hand on her shoulder. "Charley, enough's enough. You've already accused one innocent person today."

"And you're always crying wolf," Terry added. "Kay, I can vouch for Joel's innocence. In my opinion, Charley is the paranoid lunatic that should be locked up."

"Well, *I* don't trust any man who beats up a girl." Kay's eyes blazed. "Vince, radio a technician to check the lift."

Vince nodded, thumbed his mic and made the call.

"I was in the middle of fixing it," protested Joel, his hand still pressed to his bearded jaw.

"He's lying again!" cried Charley. "Look at him! He's got guilt written all over his face."

For the first time, Kay properly looked at the roadie's face. Her eyes widened. "I know you! Your name's not Joel!"

Dropping his hand from his face, the roadie snarled, "Screw you, Kay!"

Shrugging off Terry, he pounced on the music manager. His fingers dug into her throat as he slammed her against the wall. Big T and Rick were on him in seconds. But the roadie refused to let go. Charley stepped in and side-kicked his kneecap, targeting the same one as before. There was a sickening crunch, and the roadie shrieked as he dropped to the floor.

"Good kick, Charley," grunted Big T as he and Rick pinned the man down.

Running a trembling hand through her red hair and flattening her creased blouse, Kay looked scornfully at the squirming roadie. "You can tell that to the police when they arrive . . . *Brandon*."

"Brandon?" said Charley, staring hard at the roadie. Now that Kay had said his name, Charley vaguely recognized the man. She'd downloaded his picture into the operation folder. He'd been slimmer, blond-haired and with stubble, unlike the dark-haired bearded man now writhing on the floor at their feet. But his steel-blue eyes were unmistakable. This was Brandon Mills, the songwriter who'd accused Ash of copying the hit "Only Raining."

Brandon squirmed in the bodyguards' grip, spitting at Kay. "Ash stole my song! My life!"

Kay regarded him with contempt. "And you broke my heart, among other things."

As she strode out of the room, her sharp stiletto just happened to stamp on his hand.

29

"I blame myself," admitted Kay, standing with Charley and Big T at the side of the stage as Ash prepared for his encore at the Oakland Oracle Arena. They'd all been unnerved to discover Terry's trusted roadie was Brandon Mills. However, since his arrest by the San Francisco police, it looked as if Ash would be safe from any further murder attempts. "If I'd joined the tour earlier, I might have recognized that psycho songwriter!"

"None of us did," said Big T, "and he was right under our noses."

Kay rounded on the veteran bodyguard. "Perhaps you should get your eyes tested?"

Big T's jaw tightened, and his nostrils flared.

"Brandon was well disguised," said Charley, coming to Big T's defense. "He fooled us all."

Charley cast her mind back. She remembered the bearded roadie descending the wire-rope ladder just before the bomb scare and spotlight accident. And he was the one who'd yelled at Jessie for handling the microphone before he set it up himself onstage. After seeing the "ashes to ashes" death threat, the police were going to review the hotel surveillance footage for any sign of Brandon before the fire. Charley had no doubt they'd find that evidence, just as they'd be able to link him to the "no more encores" letter and the backmasked threat on Ash's last single. Nor would she be surprised if the tire blowout that caused the tour bus crash had been another of his deliberate accidents. Brandon was a nasty piece of work.

A technician had inspected the toaster lift's hydraulic unit and discovered that it was primed to go off like a cannon. On its next use, the central piston would have shot straight through the platform and speared Ash like a harpooned whale. It would have been a gruesome and very painful death.

Charley wondered how anyone could become so deranged over an Ash Wild song that he wanted to kill not only Ash but anyone else who got in the way.

A single glance at the hysterical audience clamoring for an encore answered that question. There didn't appear to be a sane person in the whole venue. With mad eyes, wild hair and mouths fixed in permanent screams, everyone was going crazy for the rock star as he walked out onstage and began playing his worldwide hit "Only Raining."

The familiar chimes of the song's opening riff filled the massive arena, and as the crowd roared their approval Charley thought her eardrums might burst.

"Ash is on fire tonight!" remarked Kay, tapping her thigh in time to the beat of the music.

She was right. This had to be one of the best concerts of the whole tour. And though she'd missed most of it, Charley could finally enjoy Ash's performance without worrying that some tragedy was about to hit him.

Ash was safe now, his stalker destined for a lifetime in jail.

The threat of "no more encores" was no more.

Leaning close, Kay spoke above the music into Charley's ear. "You certainly lived up to your word and protected Ash. In fact, I intend to speak with Colonel Black at the end of the tour about extending your—"

From the opposite wing, they both saw Ash dash onto the stage.

But that was impossible, since Ash was already performing.

Before Charley or anyone else could react, the new Ash shoved his other self violently off the stage. The assaulted Ash flew through the air and disappeared into the security pit. It happened so fast that many fans wondered if they'd seen it at all—especially since the band played on and their idol still stood on the stage, haloed in a spotlight, no break in his performance. But when the new Ash began singing, it was obvious to everyone that he was a fraud.

Sprinting over, Charley leaped down from the stage, reaching the real Ash at the same time as the other security guards. He lay in a heap, having fallen headfirst more than six feet onto the concrete floor.

"I think I've broken my neck!" Ash gasped.

Charley knelt down beside him.

"Keep still," she whispered. "We'll call an ambulance." Tears clouded her vision, and her throat choked with a sob. After all she'd been through that night, she'd failed to protect him from the forgotten threat—Pete.

"I don't need an ambulance," explained Ash. "I need a new guitar."

He held up his busted instrument, its neck cocked at a severe angle, only held on by the steel strings. "I had to let it go to break my fall."

Charley burst into relieved laughter and hugged him. "I thought you were really hurt."

"Nah, I'm fine," said Ash, sitting up.

She helped the dazed rock star back to his feet. Onstage, Big T had seized Pete in a headlock, and the band finally stopped playing.

"I *am* Ash!" declared the boy, struggling in Big T's crushing grip. "*He's* the impostor!" He pointed an accusing finger at Ash in the pit with Charley.

"Save it, Pete. We all heard your lame attempt to sing," said Big T.

"But . . . I've got a sore throat from the fire," Pete pleaded as he was dragged away.

Ash clambered back onstage to the rapturous applause of his fans. Shouldering a new guitar, he joked to them, "Fame must have gone to his head!"

As the audience laughed, Charley called up from the pit, "You sure you're okay to go back on?"

Ash nodded and grinned. "You'd have to *kill* me to stop me doing an encore."

30

As the tour bus headed south on Interstate-5 to Los Angeles the following day, Kay called a meeting in the upper-front lounge. Ash, Charley, Big T and Terry settled themselves into the leather sofas while Vince and Rick stood with the band to hear the update on Ash's demented double.

"The doctor says Pete is suffering from grandiose delusions," Kay explained. "The boy is convinced he's Ash Wild. No one can persuade him otherwise."

"What if he is? And we've got the wrong one?" The bassist scrutinized the Ash sitting beside Charley on the sofa.

Ash's lip curled. "Ha ha! We'd soon know if *you* were replaced. The bass playing would be better!"

"Harsh!" The drummer laughed, punching the bassist's arm at Ash's joke.

Kay silenced them with a glare. "According to the doctor, Pete has a history of mental health issues, usually kept in check with medication. But it appears he's been forgetting to take his."

"Where's Pete now?" asked Charley.

"He's being held in a secure psychiatric clinic," Kay replied. She turned to Ash. "The question is, do you want to press charges?"

Ash gazed through the window at the passing traffic. "Pete did me a favor. As my decoy, he gave me the space that I needed." Ash glanced fondly at Charley, who felt an unexpected flush rise in her cheeks. She still wore the white-gold bracelet he'd bought her in Las Vegas. "Besides, I wasn't hurt badly. Let's call it quits."

Kay looked surprised. "That's your final decision?"

Ash shrugged a yes. "He's a superfan, and they can all get a little crazy sometimes."

"Fine. I'll let the clinic know, so he can be sent back to the UK." Her tone hardened. "But what *I* want to know is how a mentally disturbed fan was allowed backstage in the first place."

Her eyes raked across Vince, Rick and Charley before settling on Big T. Just as she was about to rip into the veteran bodyguard, Ash cut in. "That was my idea," he admitted. "As I said, Pete made a great decoy."

"Still," said Kay, her glare returning to its original target, "it was Big T's responsibility to security-check *everyone* on the tour."

"I did do a background check on Pete. It came up with nothing," said Big T.

"Well, you obviously didn't do it thoroughly enough," said Kay. "How could you miss—"

"I got the same result when I ran a separate check," Charley interrupted, trying to take the heat off Big T as he'd so often done for her. "There'd been a huge database crash, and Pete's medical records were corrupted. From what was available, he appeared normal, aside from his obvious fixation on Ash." She held up a picture on her phone of a room wreathed from floor to ceiling in Ash Wild memorabilia. "Pete posted this online. As you can see, his bedroom's a virtual shrine to Ash."

"Jeez, that guy is beyond a superfan! It's creepy," remarked the bassist. "He's even got Ash Wild duvet covers! Now, that *is* terrifying."

Kay stabbed a gold-ringed finger at the photo. "Shouldn't *that* have rung alarm bells?"

Charley winced at the sharpness of her tongue. "Like Big T, I was always suspicious of Pete, but his room isn't any different from countless other fans' bedrooms around the world."

"That may be so"—Kay turned on Big T again—"but Pete was the *second* danger to slip through your fingers last night."

The bodyguard puffed up his chest. "Kay, we *all* missed Brandon. Terry hired him! Even defended him, for heaven's sake!" The tour manager said nothing, but shrank into the sofa, hoping not to attract Kay's wrath. "Brandon was a devious psychopath. He altered his appearance, faked his ID and credentials, and even fooled *you* for a while."

"It still amounts to a major oversight in security," snapped Kay. "You and I will revisit this issue at the end of the tour. In the meantime, please reassure me that it's within your capability to keep Ash alive for the final two dates in L.A."

Big T bristled, but he kept his cool. "Yes," he said through clenched teeth. "I'll guard Ash with my life. He's safe as houses."

31

"Ash, five minutes to showtime!" called Terry, knocking on his dressing-room door at the Staples Center in downtown Los Angeles.

Charley and Big T stood on either side of the door, ready to escort Ash to the stage.

Security was super tight. No one was allowed in or out without a pass, and faces were being checked against computer records. The entire security team was on duty and in a state of heightened alert. Only an hour before Ash was due to perform, Kay had received a disturbing call from the San Francisco police. Brandon Mills had escaped earlier that morning after the vehicle taking him to the courthouse was involved in an accident. An official manhunt was now under way.

On hearing the news, a heated argument broke out among the team about whether to go ahead with the gig. But Ash had been adamant that he wouldn't be terrorized into canceling. These were the final two dates of his sold-out tour, his fans were waiting and he *wouldn't* disappoint them. Terry had backed this decision, pointing out that Brandon's pass had been confiscated. And, after repeated reassurances from Big T that his security could handle the threat, Kay had reluctantly agreed.

Terry glanced at his watch impatiently. "Ash?" he called. He was about to knock again when the door opened and Ash emerged, sunglasses on and stage ready.

"You all right?" asked Terry.

"Yeah," replied Ash, his voice still hoarse from the fire. "Just a little nervous, that's all."

"No need to be," said Charley, offering him an encouraging smile even though she was as tense as a wire. "You're safe as houses."

Big T shot her a sideways look. "Now you're stealing all my lines!"

Surrounded by his entourage, Ash made his way along the corridor toward the stage like a prize fighter about to enter the arena. No one could have gotten near the rock star. Any attacker would have to battle through a first ring of bodyguards, then tackle Big T and his legendary right hook, after which they'd still face Charley, the final invisible ring of defense.

Of course, Brandon Mills knew from experience that Charley was someone to be reckoned with, and he might even suspect she was Ash's personal bodyguard. But now that the whole team knew who Brandon was, every eye in the place would be on the lookout for him.

As they approached the auditorium, the entourage split. Ash headed beneath the stage with Big T to the toaster lift, while Charley and the other bodyguards peeled off to take up strategic posts around the venue. Stationed in the wings, Charley peered out at the stage to be confronted by an endless sea of faces. Once more the task ahead seemed insurmountable.

How am I supposed to spot a killer in a crowd of fifty thousand screaming fans?

Her eyes scanned the front rows of frenzied teenage girls, embarrassingly excited moms, pockets of rocker boys and a handful of reluctant fathers dragged along yet secretly thrilled by a live rock concert. The lack of adults, Charley realized, should make it easier to spot a lone man in the crowd. But she couldn't take anyone for granted. Brandon had already shown a cunning talent for disguise.

As her gaze swept the audience, Charley spied a familiar ratty face in the press pit.

Gonzo.

How has he, of all paps, snagged a press pass for the final shows? she wondered.

Then the house lights went down and the video screens began their countdown. The crowd shouted along, cheering as the number one flashed up on the monitors and a huge explosion rumbled through the arena. The cascade of red and gold sparks lit up the stage like a supernova and the gut-thumping throb of a heartbeat blasted out of the speakers.

At that moment Charley was blind and deaf to any threats.

The sound of a blazing fire grew, and the silhouette of a winged boy flitted from screen to screen until consumed by the flames.

INDESTRUCTIBLE . . . IMPOSSIBLE . . . I'M POSSIBLE!

Charley felt her stomach clench as a thunderclap heralded Ash's dramatic entrance. From now on until the end of the concert, Ash would be exposed and unguarded on the stage.

Charley could only watch, hope . . . and react.

Shooting up from the toaster lift, Ash flew through the air and landed to the sound of euphoric screaming. He stood, legs astride, relishing the adulation.

Then Ash pumped a fist in the air and cried, "What's up, Los Ang—"

But he didn't finish the sentence. On the massive screens overhead, in full glorious definition, every fan watched in horror as a spurt of blood burst from Ash's chest.

32

Charley was running before Ash even hit the ground. At first she thought she was experiencing déjà vu, a flashback to when the spotlight had almost crushed Ash. But then reality struck. She'd seen the red laser dot—a second too late.

Charley was first at Ash's side, shielding his body from whatever attack might come next. He lay in a pool of his own blood, spluttering and writhing in pain. His sunglasses dislodged, hazel eyes bulging, he caught sight of Charley and desperately tried to focus on her face.

"H-h-help!" he gasped, clasping her wrist.

"Don't try to speak," said Charley as she rapidly assessed his condition. His shirt was soaked with blood, his breathing wet and rapid, and his pulse erratic.

Ripping off his top to examine the damage, Charley discovered a small round puncture wound in his upper-right chest.

A bullet hole.

Big T, now at her side, barked into his mic. *"Gunshot confirmed. Secure all exits. Suspect armed and dangerous."*

In her earpiece, Charley heard a burst of security chatter. More and more people crowded around the bleeding body. Kay, Terry, Zoe, Jessie, band members, roadies . . . even Gonzo, who'd broken through the security line determined to capture the money shot that would become the defining image for the world's media. In the background, Charley was dimly aware of chaos in the arena, fans screaming and panicked parents fleeing with their children in their arms.

The venue's medic appeared with a first-aid kit and dropped down opposite Charley.

Ash was now panting rapidly, each breath more strained. His chest barely moved, and there was a blue tinge to his lips.

"Oh my!" exclaimed the medic, turning pale at the profusion of blood.

When he failed to act, and simply stared at the dying rock star, Charley took the situation into her own hands. "Give me your med-kit," she ordered.

In his shocked state, he handed it over. Rummaging through the bag, Charley found a large-bore needle with a one-way valve and tore off the sterilized wrapper.

"What are you doing?" the medic cried, suddenly aware that a teenage girl was about to perform a serious medical procedure.

"He's suffering a tension pneumothorax," explained Charley, locating the second intercostal space on Ash's chest. "His injured lung will collapse and he'll die if we don't release the pressure."

Placing the sharp point against his skin, Charley prayed her diagnosis was correct and that she wouldn't puncture any vital organs. But there was no time to hesitate. Ash's life was on a knife's edge. She drove the needle in at ninety degrees. Ash was in too much pain to notice it slide between his ribs and penetrate deep into his chest cavity. As the valve opened, a sharp hiss of air was heard and Ash's breathing immediately eased.

But the medical emergency wasn't over yet. In her head Charley ran through *Dr. ABC* again. Big T was dealing with the danger. Ash was still responsive. His airway and breathing were stabilized, at least for the time being. But, judging by the ever-expanding pool of blood on the stage, Ash's circulation was the critical issue now.

Kay was on the phone to the emergency services. *"Of course he has insurance! Just send a bloody helicopter!"*

"He needs fluids," said Charley urgently.

The medic nodded and took out a pouch of saline solution, a sterile tube and a cannula. With practiced efficiency, he inserted the cannula into Ash's forearm, while Charley set to work bandaging and sealing the open chest wound.

Yet, despite all their efforts, Ash's condition continued to deteriorate. His breathing was shallow, his heart rate more erratic than ever. Then suddenly his eyes rolled back in their sockets and his head flopped to the side.

"Ash! Stay with us!" cried Charley, shaking his shoulder. "The ambulance is on its way."

But Ash no longer responded. Charley looked to the medic for help.

"Possible internal bleeding," he said, noticing the saline solution was already three-quarters empty. "Little we can do until we get him to a hospital."

He took out the other saline pouch in the med-kit, but as he was attaching it to the drip, Charley noticed Ash had stopped breathing altogether. The medic checked his pulse. "His heart's stopped!"

The two of them immediately commenced CPR, the medic administering chest compressions while Charley delivered the rescue breaths. They were still going when two paramedics arrived on the scene.

Exhausted and emotionally drained, Charley didn't put up any resistance as the paramedics took over.

Not long after their initial assessment and attempts at resuscitation, the older of the two spoke to his colleague: "Record time of death as twenty-sixteen hours. Cause of death: gunshot trauma."

The words hit Charley like a punch to the guts. For a moment, she simply stared at the paramedic, imagining . . .

hoping . . . praying she'd heard wrong. Ash *couldn't* be dead.

"I'm sorry for your loss," said the paramedic as he ran through the routine death-declaration procedure.

As Kay stifled a sob, her knees went weak and Terry had to support her. Big T stood motionless and silent as a rock. Charley clutched Ash's lifeless hand in her own and wept.

Gradually she became aware of a heartless photographer snapping away right next to her, capturing her grief from every angle.

Charley could take no more.

"You vulture!" she spat at him. "Have you no respect?"

Zooming his lens in on her tearstained face, Gonzo answered with another flash of his camera.

33

Big T wrapped Charley in one of his massive arms and led her away from the frenzy of photographers that had now descended on the stage.

"Charley, you did all that you could for Ash," he said, his voice on the point of cracking. "But we still have a job to do."

Stunned with grief, Charley barely heard him. Ash was unique among all the boys she'd ever met. And only now did she realize how much he'd worked his way into her heart. She felt another hole of grief open up next to those for her parents and Kerry.

"Brandon's somewhere in this building, and we have to hunt him down," said Big T fiercely. "We owe it to Ash to find his killer."

Charley gazed at the white-gold bracelet on her wrist, now glittering against the blood from Ash's wound. Her sorrow turned to anger: Brandon would pay. He *couldn't* be allowed to escape. Leaving the stage, she took a last glance back at her rock star. The paparazzi buzzed like flies over his dead body as the paramedic removed the cannula from Ash's tattooed arm.

Then it hit her. "That's not Ash!"

"Charley, don't fool yourself," said Big T softly. "Denial is a natural stage of the grie—"

"Ash's phoenix tattoo is on his *left* arm, not his right!" she cut in.

Big T's bald head swiveled around like an owl's, and he stared at the body lying on the stage. *"Sweet Mother of Mercy!"*

"That's got to be Pete," said Charley, at once saddened and elated at her discovery. "Which means . . . Ash must be at the psychiatric clinic."

Big T's thick brow creased into a frown as he tried to get his head around this. "Keep it quiet until I've got confirmation from the clinic. We don't want to raise anyone's hopes . . . or alert Brandon to his mistake."

As Big T stepped away to tell Kay, Charley spotted Gonzo heading backstage. She wondered what the little creep was sticking his nose into now. Then a thought struck her. On his camera he probably had photos of the moments running up to Ash's—or Pete's—murder. This might give vital clues about where the gunshot had come from and Brandon's location, even his possible escape route.

Maybe Gonzo could prove useful for once.

"Hey, Gonzo!" called Charley, hurrying after him.

But he didn't seem to hear. Pushing through the blackout curtains, she saw his wiry figure disappear down a corridor. *Why is he in such a rush?* she wondered.

She chased him through the warren of backstage tunnels, always several steps behind. He rounded a corner, and when she reached it, Gonzo was nowhere in sight.

Then she heard a door click shut at the far end of the hallway. Dashing down to the door marked BAY D: AUTHORIZED PERSONNEL ONLY, she barged her way through into a darkened loading bay. Gonzo was scurrying across the concrete toward an as-yet-unsecured exit.

"Hey, Gonzo, hold up!" she shouted.

Startled, the pap guy froze and turned, as if caught in the beam of a searchlight, but immediately relaxed when he saw Charley. "If it isn't Ash's guardian angel," he sneered. "Not much left to guard now, huh?"

Charley ignored the cruel taunt. "Where do you think you're going?" she demanded, running over to him.

"None of your business."

"I think it is. The venue's in lockdown."

"I've got to take these photos to my agency *right now*," he snapped. "If I don't, I'll miss the scoop of a lifetime."

"Can I have a look first?" Charley asked.

Gonzo blinked. "Not on your life."

"I'm not going to delete them," she said, reaching out to the camera dangling around his neck. "They could hold clues to identify the gunman."

Gonzo clasped the camera to his chest as if she were asking him to hand over his own baby.

"I only want to look," insisted Charley. "Surely you owe me that."

"I owe you nothing!" he spat, turning to leave.

Big T's voice sounded in her earpiece. *"Charley, where are you?"*

"In loading bay D," she responded into her mic.

"Security upda . . ." Interference broke up the signal. *"Caught . . . in San Jose . . . killer is . . ."*

"Say again," said Charley, clasping a hand to her ear.

"The killer isn't Brandon."

34

"Stop!" Charley cried as Gonzo reached the emergency exit. "You're not going anywhere."

Gonzo swiveled around to face her.

"How about a last shot?" he said, pointing his camera at Charley. "The grieving girlfriend."

"Gonzo, I don't have time to play games," said Charley. "You might have evidence of the killer. Hand it over."

Gonzo adjusted the flashgun on his camera. "Smile for the birdy!"

Charley noticed the little red laser dot on her chest a moment too late. *The flashgun was a real gun!*

Gonzo's finger pressed the shutter button. Charley braced herself for the impact . . . There was a click but no flash.

With a blast of expletives, Gonzo furiously tapped away at the button.

"Run out of film?" asked Charley, diving forward to tackle him before he could clear the jam.

Gonzo tried to bat her away with his camera. The flash caught her a glancing blow on the cheek, but she managed to pin him against the wall. As she tried to wrestle the lethal camera off him, Gonzo grabbed her hair and yanked her head backward. She gave a shriek as he tugged mercilessly. Before she could tear herself free of his grip, he whipped her head to the side and she collided, bone to brick, against the wall. Stars burst across her vision, her skull rang like a bell and she was forced to let him go.

Taking advantage of her dazed state, Gonzo swept her legs from under her. Charley fell to the floor, where he roundly kicked her in the stomach. Winded and retching up bile, Charley lay gagging for breath, pain racking her body. She heard the scrape of metal and saw Gonzo picking up a crowbar from the top of a crate.

"I said you'd live to regret your actions, *angel*."

As Gonzo raised the crowbar to deliver a killing blow, Charley gasped, "Ash isn't dead!"

"What?"

"You shot his decoy."

"You're lying."

But the hesitation in his attack was all she needed.

Fight smarter, not harder.

Charley drove her fist into his groin—always a woman's smartest move in self-defense.

Gonzo yelped like a wounded puppy and dropped to the floor, the crowbar clattering to the concrete. As he knelt with his hands clasped between his legs, she slammed her palm into the bridge of his crooked nose. There was a satisfying crunch, and blood streamed from his nostrils. Stunned and in obvious pain, Gonzo hissed and bared his teeth like a cornered rat. He lashed out at her with a fist, but she caught his hand and spiraled it into a wristlock. Applying pressure, Charley forced him to the ground, where he lay squirming like a pinned beetle.

Though restrained, Gonzo still struggled and spat at her. Charley took hold of his index finger. Any further injury, she reasoned, could be blamed on his own force in resisting.

"I assume this is the trigger finger you use to take your vile photos?" she said coolly. "So I suggest you keep still."

She applied an extra-hard twist to his wrist to drive home her warning.

Wincing, Gonzo glared up at her and snarled, "Shove it, Wildcat!"

Charley smiled, then wrenched the finger all the way back. A sickening crack resounded through the loading bay, swiftly followed by Gonzo's agonized scream, just as Big T and two other security guards burst through the door.

"I *told* you to keep still," she said, confident her action was *necessary*, *reasonable* and *proportional* to the pain and suffering he'd inflicted on her and Ash.

Big T came running over, stared at the deformed finger, then smirked at Gonzo. "Well, you won't be taking any shots for a very long time!"

35

"It's an impressive piece of equipment," remarked the officer in charge, inspecting the flashgun weapon before it was bagged for evidence. "Criminals are becoming more inventive every day."

He sipped from a coffee cup and grimaced at the taste. "Man, that's gross! Don't they have any decent coffee in this venue?"

Tossing the cup into a nearby trash can, he turned to Charley and Big T in the loading bay. They'd given their statements and were just waiting to be dismissed. "I think we're done here. That was pretty brave of you, young lady, to tackle the suspect alone. But next time leave it to the professionals, like your bodyguard friend here. Without proper training, you could easily have been killed."

Charley said nothing. Big T suppressed a knowing grin.

"She's a psycho! A wildcat! *She broke my finger!*" bawled

Gonzo as he was bundled into a police car. "You should be arresting her, not me!"

The officer in charge snorted. "Why is it that killers always think they're the victims?"

He shrugged and strode away to his car.

Charley glanced up at Big T. "Leave it to the *professionals*? What am I, then?"

"You're the real thing," Big T replied. "Just a pity you didn't break *all* his fingers."

Charley responded with a strained smile.

"Hey, I certainly would have!" admitted the veteran bodyguard. "Now, come on—we should update the others."

Charley followed Big T back through the maze of corridors to the artists' lounge. The atmosphere among the band and road crew was subdued, though there was a buzz as Charley entered the room. She heard whispers of *"Did she really catch the killer?"*

Kay, Terry and Zoe were embroiled in a heated discussion in the tour manager's office.

"It could so easily have been Ash!" said Kay fiercely. "I'll have Big T's head for this."

"Just be thankful Brandon's been recaptured," replied Terry. "At least he's no longer a threat."

"But we were looking for the wrong guy! And now Ash is locked up in a mental ward! How did we ever make that mis—" She broke off as Big T knocked at the door and entered.

"Charley! Are you all right?" Kay asked with genuine concern, ignoring Big T as he closed the door behind them.

"Just about," Charley replied, still feeling the throb in her gut where Gonzo had kicked her. "That rat Gonzo tried to shoot me with his camera, *literally*."

"Gonzo's a murdering scumbag," said Big T. "But he's now where he belongs. Behind bars."

Kay shot him a fierce glare. "Only thanks to Charley here. I thought *you* promised to protect Ash with your life."

"It *wasn't* Ash," argued the bodyguard, folding his arms defensively.

Kay sneered. "Lucky for you."

"What I don't understand is why Gonzo would want to kill Ash in the first place," said Zoe, frowning.

"He needed the money," replied Big T.

"What money?" asked Terry.

"The fees he'd earn from his photos to pay off his gambling debt to the mob."

"If that's the case, why didn't you identify Gonzo as a threat before?" demanded Kay.

"He was," said Big T, holding her accusative glare. "None of us ever imagined, though, he'd go to *these* lengths to engineer a 'unique' photo. He'd bugged Ash's hotel room, tried to incite him to violence, even caused our car crash in New Orleans—I traced the registration plate of the motorbike back to him. These tactics are typical of the paparazzi. But after photographing the fire in San Francisco, it seems he was inspired to murder by Brandon."

"Brandon?" exclaimed Kay.

"Yes," said Charley, joining in the discussion. "It bothered me that Gonzo was always in the wrong place at the wrong time. It was as if he knew about the accidents in advance. We suspect he and Brandon made a deal. Brandon set up the accidents, and Gonzo captured them on film."

"So, when Brandon was caught, Gonzo took things into his own hands," continued Big T. "You see, to kill Ash would be the ultimate payoff in terms of a money shot. It would be like catching the moment John Lennon was murdered."

"But he'd be killing the golden goose," remarked Terry.

Big T nodded. "Yeah, but he'd have made his fortune. Photos of Ash dying would have been sold around the world and earned him millions."

"And how is Ash?" asked Charley. In all the craziness, she'd yet to ask about him. "I need to see him."

"I gave the clinic a call, but it's past office hours," replied Kay. "The night-duty nurse had an emergency number for the doctor in charge, so I'm waiting for a call back."

At that moment her phone rang. She snatched it up and listened. "You're absolutely certain?" she asked, before listening some more. "Thank you, Doctor."

Frowning, Kay put her phone down. "The doctor says the client was escorted to the airport, checked in and taken through to the departure lounge. But it appears he never got on the flight to England. What's really odd, though, is the doctor insists the tattoo was on his right arm. They definitely had Pete, *not* Ash, in their care."

Charley stared at Big T. "So where's Ash?"

36

"No more encores? You've got to be kidding. This is my third!" yelled the teen rock star, running back onstage to earsplitting screams and thunderous applause on the final night of the Indestructible tour.

And what a perfect name for the tour it is, thought Charley. For someone who'd been threatened with death, almost crushed by a spotlight, suffered an electric shock by a mic, trapped by a hotel fire, thrown off the stage and, finally, tied up and blindfolded by his doppelgänger, Ash had an amazing resilience—fueled, it seemed, by the undying devotion of his fans.

After a frantic search of the Staples Center, they'd found Ash bound and gagged inside a locked wardrobe in his dressing room. He'd been in the venue the whole time. According to Ash, Pete had caught a flight down to L.A. and then taken a taxi to the Staples Center. After conning his way into the venue as Ash, he'd waited in the dressing room. Ash had been taken by surprise, tied up and shoved in the wardrobe by Pete.

On his release, Ash had been furious. But when he discovered Pete's fate, he was first shocked and then thankful that his decoy had saved him from that fatal shot. After hearing about Charley's encounter with Gonzo, his concern focused on her, but Charley assured him she was fine. She was his bodyguard, and it was all part of the job.

Kay had launched a demonic investigation into how Pete slipped past security, but gradually calmed down once she knew that Ash was alive and well. With Brandon back in custody, Gonzo behind bars and Pete lying in a morgue, Ash was no longer the target of any known death threats. All the same, everyone on the security team remained alert and on edge for his final concert.

Miraculously, the gig went well—with just one small hitch at the end.

"I've got no more songs!" Ash admitted, spreading his arms wide in apology to his insatiable fans.

There was an arena-sized groan.

He smiled. "Perhaps . . . I do have *one* more."

A huge cheer rocked the venue.

"It's brand-new. Not even my band has heard it," said Ash, perching on a stool and taking an acoustic guitar from a roadie. After a strum to check that it was tuned, he reached out to adjust the mic stand . . . and stopped himself. He glanced offstage at a small group of sound technicians. "This one's safe, isn't it, guys?"

Like a group of dutiful meerkats, they all nodded their heads, then laughed at Ash's joke.

"This song is inspired by a very special girl in my life," Ash announced. "It's called 'Angel Without Wings.'"

The audience hushed into near silence as Ash plucked a bittersweet melody from his guitar. With a soulful voice that belied his young age, he began to sing. *"Time will heal, yet memories scar, when the hurt's so deep, a bridge too far . . ."*

Once more Charley felt her eyes well up with tears and her throat constrict.

"In times of trouble, I need a helping hand. I look for you, breathe for you, have a need for you . . ."

Ash looked in Charley's direction. His eyes met hers as he sang the chorus.

"You lift me up, lift me up. Make all my troubles fade away . . ."

For Charley, the whole arena faded to nothing. It was as if Ash was singing only to her. And only she mattered.

"There stands my angel without wings. Who needs wings . . . to be an angel?"

37

"That's a number-one hit!" declared Kay, hugging Ash as he joined them in the artists' lounge for the after-show party. She was beside herself with excitement. "We must get you in the studio as soon as we're back. It's all about the moment—and you've captured it!"

Charley was equally overcome with emotion. Still reeling from being serenaded with her very own song, she walked alongside Ash as if floating on air. For the first time in years, her heart felt full—untroubled, complete, at peace.

But she wouldn't get a moment alone with Ash to thank him for quite a while yet. Band members, road crew, invited guests and media were all lined up to congratulate and compliment him. Ash beamed and nodded his thanks, basking in the praise. After all the storms he'd weathered, Charley felt he deserved his time in the sun.

Stepping away from the throng of well-wishers, Charley spotted Jessie standing alone and apart from the others. The fan-club organizer had been quiet and withdrawn ever since Charley had accused her of trying to kill Ash. The two of them had not spoken a word to each other since. Realizing there'd never be a good time to apologize with the tour ending, this seemed like the best opportunity. Steeling herself, Charley went over to the buffet table, picked up a plate and pretended to browse the food on offer. Spring rolls, gourmet pizza slices, fancy sandwiches, chicken-satay skewers and other finger foods all surrounded a massive tiered cake decorated with candles and the word INDESTRUCTIBLE in icing.

"Hi, Jessie," she said, as lightly as she could.

Jessie ignored her.

"Listen . . . I'm sorry for what I said."

Jessie shot her a hostile stare. "Oh, you're sorry, are you? A little late for that."

"Please understand—"

"No, I understand all right," Jessie snapped, rounding on her. "It's not enough for you to steal Ash's heart. You have to break mine too."

"That wasn't my intention."

"Wasn't it? You accused me, of all people, of trying to kill Ash!" she said, her mouth twisted into a furious snarl. "Ever since we met, you've wanted me off this tour. When Ash was upset, you pushed me away. You wanted him all to yourself." Charley saw Jessie pick up a large knife from the buffet table. "You're always following him around, never letting him out of your sight. Wherever he goes, you go! You're like his shadow. The poor guy can't even breathe without you at his back. I don't know how he stands it."

Charley took a step away. "I said, I'm sorry. I was just doing my job."

"*Job?* Being Ash's girlfriend isn't a job!" exclaimed Jessie in outrage, waving the blade in Charley's face. "And from what I've seen, you don't have a clue what PR is either. What I do for Ash is a real publicity job. I've slaved on his fan website night and day, built up his following in this country from *nothing*. I've never asked for thanks. Never asked for anything. I do this because of the love I carry in my heart for him. But still he loves you more. He even writes a song for you!"

She thrust the tip of the knife accusingly at her. Charley didn't like where this was going and reached for her phone.

"It doesn't surprise me you've had death threats," Jessie went on, still waving the gleaming blade around. "You deserve all the hate you get online. I just wish I'd written some of it. 'Cause that's how I feel about you!"

As Jessie raised the knife, Charley thrust her iStun into the girl's gut. Jessie's whole body convulsed and jerked as three million volts of electricity coursed through her system. The shock was too much for her, and she passed out, dropping to the carpet in a heap.

People were quick to notice, and Ash came dashing over

with everyone else. "What's happened to Jessie?" he asked.

Not wanting to make any more of a scene, Charley quietly pocketed her phone and shrugged. "Jessie must have been . . . overcome by your performance. She just fainted."

"Poor Jessie," said Ash as Big T knelt down beside the unconscious girl and tried to revive her. "She was so looking forward to cutting the end-of-tour cake with me."

38

"You stunned her for trying to cut a cake!" Jason exclaimed during her video call to Guardian HQ the next morning from her hotel room on Sunset Boulevard. He laughed. "I got away lightly with a dislocated finger, then."

"You won't ever forgive me for that, will you?" said Charley, her cheeks reddening with shame at her overreaction in using the iStun—the fangirl might have been angry with her, but not to the point of murder.

"Hey, I deserved that," said Jason. Charley saw him glance around the briefing room, then lean closer to the webcam. In a lowered voice, he said, "Listen, I know we got off on the wrong foot, Charley, and we haven't exactly been best of friends, but I think it's time I gave you an apology."

"For what?" asked Charley.

"For being a jerk!"

Charley was rendered speechless by his stark self-assessment.

"I was . . ." Jason seemed to struggle for the right words. "*Wrong* to assume just because you're a girl you'd be no good as a bodyguard. After seeing you in action on this operation—palm-striking guys, resuscitating Principals and taking down not just one but *two* maniacs—it's obvious you're as capable as any of us boys, if not more so." He smiled. "Can we start over?"

Charley realized how much Jason must have swallowed his pride to admit this. And, despite their history, she found it easy to forgive and forget. "Of course," she said. "And I'm sorry for dislocating your finger."

"No worries, they still all work." Jason wiggled his fingers in front of the camera. "Besides, it was my fault. I shouldn't have been so tough on you during training."

"Yes, you should have," Charley said, to his surprise. "It was your fight-or-fail attitude that pushed me to go beyond my limits. I have a lot to thank you for. The fact you didn't make any allowances for me during training prepared me for the real world—a world that makes no allowances whatsoever."

"Well, if I'd known that," said Jason, grinning, "I'd have been an even bigger jerk!"

Charley laughed. "No, you're big enough as it is."

"Thanks! And you're one *kick-butt* bodyguard," he replied warmly. "I'm proud to be on your team. Well . . . until I get my own team!"

"Is that still happening?" she asked. Having bonded with Jason at long last, the thought of splitting up the original team saddened her.

Jason nodded. "As soon as you return from this assignment." He glanced off camera, then back at her. "Hey, the colonel wants to speak to you."

Jason left his seat, and Colonel Black's craggy face appeared on her screen.

"Outstanding work, Charley. It seems your suspicions were right about Brandon and Gonzo," he said. "The police have found evidence of coded text messages on the pap's phone. They contain times and locations that match the accidents and attacks on Ash."

"I knew it!" said Charley.

"It certainly explains how Gonzo popped up at every disaster on this tour," Colonel Black continued. "And you've done well to keep Ash alive through it all. Operation Starstruck has been an unexpectedly tough assignment. But, as you've discovered, fame is a killer."

39

Once known as the Riot House, the hotel on Sunset Boulevard was legendary among rock stars. In the 1960s and 1970s, it held the likes of The Doors, The Who and the Rolling Stones. Led Zeppelin would rent as many as six floors and stage motorcycle races in the hallways. The Who's Keith Moon threw a TV out of the window, setting a trend that John Bonham, Keith Richards and countless other rock gods followed. Lemmy of Hawkwind wrote the classic track "Motorhead" in the middle of the night on one of the hotel balconies. Jim Morrison even hung from a window once by his fingertips, causing a traffic jam in the street below. The Riot House was *the* place to hang out and party.

Tonight it hosted the official Indestructible end-of-tour party. The rooftop was buzzing with celebrities, models, musicians and movie stars. Roadies wandered around wearing T-shirts saying I SURVIVED A **WILD** TOUR! And security was so tight that even the most famous faces had to produce ID and guest invitations.

Charley, in a strapless white top and black leather jeans, was standing with Ash by the pool when all of a sudden screams of laughter burst from the direction of the bar. Having removed his sunglasses, the bassist had two black rings around his eyes. Everyone stared and pointed at the musician's bizarre appearance.

"What? *WHAT?*" he asked irritably.

"Looking good, Panda Eyes!" scoffed the drummer.

A young lady took a makeup mirror from her bag and showed the bassist his painted face. The bassist's eyes widened into hoops of astonished horror. He checked his sunglasses, his fingers coming away with black ink on them.

"Who did this?" he demanded angrily, looking around like a crazed lemur and causing more ripples of laughter to spread among the guests. *"WHO did this?!"*

Ash turned to Charley. "It wasn't me, but I wish I'd thought of that."

Charley, fighting to keep her face straight, replied, "Looks like permanent ink to me. That'll take a while to come off."

Ash closely studied her poker-faced expression. "I think I'd better keep a close eye on you from now on."

Charley laughed. It had been a long time coming, but she'd finally gotten her revenge for their prank on her at the start of the tour. She couldn't bring herself to set up Ash, but the band members were still fair game.

The party soon lost interest in the bassist and his black-ringed eyes, conversation resumed and the DJ upped the music volume. A group of girls—superfans who'd won a competition to meet their idol—approached Ash.

"Can we have your autograph, please?" asked one of the girls, presenting their party invites for signing.

"Sure," said Ash. "Do you have a pen?"

When the girl began searching in her bag, Charley produced her own pen from her back pocket—she'd come prepared this time. Ash autographed the invites with a flourish, then handed them back.

"Yours too, Charley," insisted the girl, with a hopeful smile.

"Me?" questioned Charley, blinking in surprise.

The girl nodded. "You're a real inspiration. We all want to be Wildcats like you!"

Taking the pen back from Ash, Charley signed her name next to his. Then the girls huddled close for a round of selfies with her.

"Looks like you're becoming a star yourself," Ash remarked as the girls trotted away, delighted with their collection of autographs and photos. "Before you become too famous, there's something I need to say."

Taking her hand, Ash led her to a gazebo in the far corner

of the rooftop garden. With the guests clustered around the bar and pool, the gazebo was unoccupied, and the surrounding potted plants gave them some privacy. He stopped by the rail, where the sun was setting pink-orange over the haze of L.A.

"I see you're still wearing the bracelet," he said, the woven bands of white gold gleaming on her wrist in the dying light.

"Of course," she replied, feeling his arms wrap around her.

Ash gazed intently into her eyes. Once more it seemed only she mattered.

"I wouldn't have survived this tour without you," he said. "And, while I wouldn't want to go through that hell again, I really don't want this tour to end."

"Why?" she asked, a little breathless.

"Because it means you'll no longer be with me. At my side."

"Surely that'll be a relief," she said, trying to make light of their parting. "The fact that you don't need constant protection anymore."

Ash shook his head. "Charley, you're my inspiration, my muse. I'll be lost without you."

He cupped the back of her neck in one hand and drew her close.

"I told you I'd break your arm if you ever tried to kiss me," she warned, but her tone was gentle and inviting.

Ash smiled. "Worth the risk."

Charley felt her resistance crumbling. "I'm not one of your groupies," she said.

"No, you're my guardian angel."

He leaned in to kiss her, and Charley knew she was about to break the cardinal rule of bodyguarding. *Never get involved with your Principal.*

The battle with her conscience didn't last long.

She gave into him, her heart ruling her head. Their lips were no more than a breath apart when she heard a whirring sound like an angry mosquito. She pulled back from the kiss. Hovering in the air, only a few feet from them, was a drone with a camera attached.

"For heaven's sake!" exclaimed Ash, glaring at the flying intrusion. "I can't even escape the paparazzi fourteen floors up!"

Charley calmly picked up a stone from one of the potted plants, judged the distance and flung it at the drone. The stone struck it dead center, cracking its casing, then rebounded and shattered one of its plastic propellers. The drone lurched sideways and plunged out of view.

Charley turned back to Ash. "Now where were we?"

"I think about *here*," said Ash, pressing his lips against hers.

Closing her eyes, Charley lost herself in his exquisite kiss.

"Ash?" called Kay, her high heels clicking across the stone paving toward the gazebo. Charley quickly broke away from their embrace. "Ah, there you are! There's someone I need you to meet."

Ash squeezed Charley's hand. "Wait here for me. I won't be long," he whispered, then went off with his manager.

Leaning against the rail, Charley gazed out over the West Hollywood skyline, the city lights twinkling like stars. Realizing she'd crossed a romantic line with Ash, she felt overwhelmed by a kaleidoscope of emotions. Was there a chance of a real relationship, or was that a farewell kiss? Could she remain his bodyguard and be his girlfriend too? Would she have to quit Guardian?

Whatever the answer, she had to face facts. Ash was a world-famous rock star with countless beautiful girls at his feet. She shouldn't read too much into a single kiss, however intense.

Her phone buzzed in her pocket. She pulled it out and glanced at the text—an Intruder alert.

40

The hotel corridor was deserted, with everyone on the roof for the party. Charley had spotted Ash and Kay talking with a famous film producer, so she decided not to disturb them. No one could access the penthouse floor without an authorized key card—so more than likely, a security guard or a hotel employee had entered Ash's suite, despite instructions not to service the room without advance notice.

Charley stood outside Ash's suite. The door was closed, and there were no signs of forced entry. The Intruder device was in place and undamaged. Taking out her spare key card, she slipped it into the lock and cautiously entered.

Subdued lighting illuminated the spacious lounge area with its deep leather sofa and private bar. The air conditioner hummed, and the distant thrum of passing traffic drifted up through the open patio doors leading to the balcony. Outside, dusk had settled, and L.A. glowed like the embers of a dying fire.

On initial inspection, the suite appeared unoccupied.

Her steps muted by the thick carpet, Charley crossed the empty lounge toward the bedroom. She peered inside. Nothing seemed to be disturbed. Ash's suitcases were on the rack, and his king-sized bed was untouched.

Then she noticed a light on in the bathroom—and a twitch of a shadow.

With ninja-like stealth, Charley approached the door and eased it open.

Big T stood with his back to her, a black marker in his hand.

On the mirror, scrawled in disturbingly familiar handwriting, were the words:

YOUR GUARDIAN ANGEL
WILL BE
YOUR ANGEL OF DEA

"What are you doing?" exclaimed Charley, shocked and confused by what she was witnessing.

Big T spun around, the black marker now clenched in his fist like a knife. On seeing Charley, he lowered his guard. "I . . . just discovered this death threat," he explained.

"But I saw *you* writing it."

Big T's weathered face hardened to stone. Then he gave her a sorrowful look. "I wish you hadn't."

He made a step toward her. Charley instinctively backed away. That's when she spotted a red block, with a cell phone taped and wired to it, perched on the basin's vanity unit. She instantly recognized the putty-like block to be PBX.

"What the hell, Big T!" she cried, her eyes widening in alarm. "I thought you were Ash's bodyguard!"

"And I always will be."

"But that"—she indicated the bomb—"looks like you're trying to *kill* him."

Big T responded with a single shake of his head. "I'm not one to kill the golden goose, like Gonzo. My job is to protect Ash. In fact it's the only job I know."

As the veteran bodyguard moved steadily toward her, Charley retreated through the bedroom into the lounge. "Then why the mirror threat and bomb?"

"Because I must remain essential to Ash's survival."

"What makes you think you aren't?"

"Kay Gibson." He scowled at the manager's name. "Charley, I'll let you in on a secret. I sent the original hoax letter bomb."

Charley almost stumbled over the sofa in shock at his confession.

"That red she-devil wanted to fire me before the tour even started!" he revealed, still advancing on her. "Thought I was too old to be a bodyguard. But I proved I wasn't by 'saving' Ash's life. It worked. My contract was renewed. She even gave me a raise!" He laughed. "Then that Brandon began sending Ash *real* death threats. That's when Kay decided to hire you." His eyes narrowed. "In fact she *insulted* me by hiring a teenage girl!"

"But you've helped me, backed me up when things went wrong!"

Big T nodded, the smile on his lips both tender and regretful. "I like you, Charley. You impressed me from the start. I've seen many wannabe bodyguards come and go in my time. Until a person's tested, you don't know them. And very few have the right stuff. But *you* do."

Charley found herself backed up against the bar. "Then why are you doing this?"

"Because you're *too* good. After defending Ash in Miami, then resuscitating him in Dallas, you started to eclipse me. And, when the student becomes greater than the teacher, the teacher must crush the student." The marker pen in Big T's fist snapped in his furious grasp. "I tried to get rid of you! Give you a way out with the first threat on your mirror. If you'd told your colonel, you'd have been reassigned. But you kept quiet. That's why I need *you* to be seen as a security risk to Ash—to fail in your duty while *I'm* the bodyguard that saves the day."

"But my assignment's over. I'm no threat to you."

"Yes, you are," he contradicted, sorrow entering his old watery eyes. "Kay's firing me. You're to be my replacement."

Charley's mouth fell open. "What?"

"She spoke to your Colonel Black this very evening about extending your contract."

Charley held up her hands. "Believe me, I had no idea about this."

"Well, you do now," growled Big T, closing in on her. "Tonight I was going to be the hero and discover the bomb. Change of plan, Charley—*you're* going to discover the bomb."

"Me?"

Big T nodded, his expression grim. "Unfortunately, you'll set it off 'by accident'—a tragic end to a promising career. But at least you'll have the consolation of dying in the line of duty."

41

Charley bolted for the door. Big T lunged forward and seized her by the arm. "Sorry, Charley, can't have you blabbing."

"Let me go!" screamed Charley as he dragged her toward the bedroom.

"Everyone thinks you and Ash are dating. So it won't be suspicious if you're found in his room," said Big T more to himself than to her.

Unable to break his iron grip, Charley pulled out her phone and pressed the volume button. Intent on shocking the traitorous bodyguard senseless, she thrust the arcing metal studs into his large gut.

"No, you don't!" said Big T, grabbing her wrist before she could make contact. "I saw what you did to Jessie."

He slammed her hand against the edge of the bar, forcing her to drop the iStun. He kicked the phone under the sofa. Despite having both hands pinned, Charley booted him hard in the shins. His eyes flared with pain, but he didn't let her go. With the practiced brutality of a bouncer, he lassoed a muscled arm around her neck and trapped her in a crushing headlock.

"Please don't struggle!" he said, his tone more imploring than angry. "You'll only make it worse for yourself."

Fighting for breath, she felt her neck being crushed in his grip. Charley reached across to Big T's hand, found his little finger and wrenched it backward. There was a sharp snap and a pained grunt. But the pressure on her throat didn't ease.

"Nice try," he hissed through clenched teeth. "But I've broken too many bones in my lifetime to worry about a little finger."

He began hauling her across the room like a giant with a doll. Charley clawed at his arm, but it was pointless. His muscles were as unyielding as steel.

"Why did you have to find me?" he muttered. "I had it all planned. No one was supposed to get hurt, especially not you. But you've forced me into this . . ."

Darkness began to seep into Charley's vision. Then she remembered the *kubotan* pen in her pocket. Seizing it like an ice pick, she drove its reinforced point into a cluster of nerves in Big T's forearm. The sudden unexpected jolt of concentrated pain ripped through him. Charley felt the headlock loosen, and she stabbed the tip into his upper thigh.

A second excruciating burst of pain caused Big T to crumple, and he dropped Charley to the floor.

"You really are a wildcat!" he raged as he hobbled to the wall for support.

Gasping for air, Charley used the bar to pull herself up. Out of the corner of her eye, she caught a flicker of movement and ducked. Big T's legendary right hook whistled a hair's breadth from her head. Knowing she wouldn't survive one of those punches, Charley grabbed a glass bottle from the bar, spun around and smashed it on Big T's bald head. Liquid and fragments of glass showered over him, but he barely flinched.

"Now the gloves are off!" he snarled, and brought a bottle hammering down toward her head. But her earlier strike had obviously had some impact, for he wasn't quite on target. The bottle caught Charley a glancing blow—enough to briefly stun and drop her, but not to knock her out. With her skull throbbing and her vision doubled, she collapsed beside the sofa.

"Now stay down!" Big T slurred, propping himself against the bar.

In her daze, Charley spotted the gleam of two metal studs beneath the sofa. Reaching out, her fingers found the edge of her phone. Desperately she tried to get a grip. Behind her, she heard a tinkle of glass and knew Big T was heading for her. He grasped the back of her top and pulled her away from the sofa.

With a hand clamped around her throat, Big T lifted her off the ground. Charley spluttered and gagged.

"You were like a daughter to me," he said, looking at her with bloodshot eyes. "Believe me, I didn't want it to end like this."

"Me neither!" she gasped, thrusting the iStun into his chest. The points contacted straight over his heart.

Big T convulsed, choked and staggered back through the open patio door.

But one jolt wasn't enough. The bodyguard was as strong as a grizzly bear. He still had her by the throat. Charley hit him again. Big T's body went into spasm. He fell backward and hit the balcony rail. It cracked under his weight. Losing his balance, Big T began to topple over the side.

He made no effort to save himself.

"I'm so sorry, Charley," he gasped, regret in his eyes as he tumbled into the darkness.

But his muscles were still locked out by the iStun—and Charley was caught in his death grip. Screaming, she was dragged over with him.

42

"The doctor tells me people who fall more than ten stories rarely survive," said Colonel Black, standing stiff and awkward beside Charley's bed in the intensive-care unit of Children's Hospital Los Angeles. "Big T died on impact, but his body broke your fall. You were extremely lucky."

Charley stared down at herself, her eyes unfocused, yet seeing all too much.

Lucky? she thought bitterly.

Her paralyzed legs were sprawled on the bed, lifeless and bizarrely misshapen. She felt sick. They looked like a scarecrow's in a horror movie, feet bent at unnatural angles. She couldn't feel them. It was as if they weren't *her* legs at all.

"Mostly it's positive news," the colonel went on, a leaden smile on his haggard face, but Charley was barely listening. "Your broken arm and cracked ribs will heal with no long-term effects. You haven't got any pelvic injuries, which is a miracle—that can be problematic, even fatal. The only serious damage from the fall is to the base of your spine, but the doctors are doing more tests."

Charley had little memory of the fall. She recalled the bright joy of the rooftop party, the thrill of her kiss with Ash and her wide-open hopes for the future. And she remembered the scrawled threat on the mirror, her deep shock and sadness at Big T's treachery and the crushing grip of his fingers around her throat. Then she had been falling . . . plunging into a deep well of blackness. Drowning in darkness, she had almost never come back up. Perhaps that would have been a blessing? For when she did surface again, she knew that not all of her had returned.

"And I guarantee you'll get the best care possible. No expense spared." The colonel paused and fished something out of his pocket. He tried to make eye contact with her and failed. "Charley, I realize this isn't much after all you've lost but . . ." He held up a small gold shield with Guardian wings. "For outstanding bravery and sacrifice in the line of duty."

When she didn't react, he swallowed uncomfortably and placed it on her bedside table.

Charley ignored the gold badge . . . and Colonel Black.

"Right. I'll return tomorrow," said the colonel, a crack in his voice. "Is there anything you want?"

YES! A pair of legs that WORK! Charley screamed in her head.

When she remained silent, Colonel Black nodded goodbye and walked out.

Charley stared at the two lumps of meat that had been her legs, now propped on the bed. In her head a single maddening question repeated over and over . . .

Will I ever walk again?

43

At first Charley grieved the loss of her legs, crying herself to sleep each pain-racked night.

In her dreams she was whole again, surfing endless oceans or running over mountains, faster and faster, her feet barely touching the ground. Then she'd wake believing she could walk, her heart light and her head happy until she tried to move. Her legs would refuse all commands. Sweat would pour from her brow as she mentally screamed at them to respond.

This denial of her disabled state didn't last long. Soon Charley grew to hate the sight of her legs. *What use were they if they didn't work?* They were like two logs of rotten wood. She could saw them off, and she wouldn't feel or notice a difference!

At the end of her first week in the hospital, she was moved from the intensive-care unit to the high-dependency unit. *Progress,* the nurse told her with a cheery smile.

It didn't feel like progress to Charley—just a different room with the same antiseptic smell and the same routine as before.

Then, in the second week, while a nurse was washing what used to be her legs, Charley felt a slight sensation of pins and needles. She still couldn't tell which leg the nurse was touching, but there was a definite feeling. She'd enthusiastically told the nurse, and a doctor had been called. But when he performed a series of sensory tests, her legs didn't react to any other stimuli. The doctor was encouraging, but Charley's spark of hope faded.

Yet a couple of days later, some sensation returned to her lower abdomen. This time the doctor was noticeably animated. *A vital neurological sign for future leg function,* he'd said. It still seemed like the thinnest of threads reconnecting her to her lower half. But it was enough to reignite Charley's hope and carry her through the long dark hours, alone and scared of what the future might hold.

The changes were small, but toward the end of the first month, Charley was convinced some feeling had returned to the soles of her feet. It was as if her legs were waking up from a decade-long hibernation. Some days she could even sense their position on the bed. At night the nerves inside buzzed, like a broken hard drive trying to reboot itself.

One glorious morning Charley discovered she could wiggle her toes. Only a fraction—but it was movement.

Then, just as she was celebrating this progress, her whole body went into spasm. It started in her legs, rushed up like a tsunami through her body, arched her spine backward and turned her hands into claws, crushing the paper cup in her grasp and sending water flying.

There was no pain. But Charley was terrified.

The spasm lasted a minute or so, yet felt like eons to Charley. When it subsided, she discovered the doctor at her side. Soothing her, he explained that spasms were a side effect of her spinal injury. Her body's normal reflex system was being short-circuited. The explanation brought Charley little relief.

One afternoon, after a particularly violent spasm, there was a knock at her door. Ash popped his head in.

"How you doing today?" he asked.

"All right," she lied, wiping perspiration from her forehead with the back of her hand.

"I've brought some more grapes and a couple of new books."

"Thanks," she replied as he put the gifts on her bedside table and pulled up a chair. He'd visited her almost every day, and this afternoon he seemed more lively than usual, his knee jittering up and down with repressed excitement.

Ash took her hand. She let him, her fingers lying in his palm as lifeless as her legs. "I know I've said this before, but

I'm so sorry about all this." He glanced down the length of the bed.

Charley forced a smile. "Pool had to be on the roof, didn't it?"

Ash's laugh was as hollow as her smile. "Hey, I'm not doing that crazy stunt ever again. Where's your phone, by the way?"

Charley nodded to the desk drawer. Pulling it open, Ash paired his own phone with hers and transferred a file. As he waited for it to download, he explained enthusiastically, "I finished recording your song last night. Finally nailed it. The producer and Kay both think the track's a classic. It's going to be the lead single off my new album—"

"Why do you keep visiting me?" Charley interrupted.

Ash blinked in surprise. "Because I want to."

"No, *really*?"

"To support you, of course. Like you looked after me. That's why I've stayed on in L.A. to record my album."

"Not because you feel obliged to . . . or guilty?"

Ash averted his eyes. "Of course I feel guilty. You were hurt protecting me."

Charley withdrew her hand. She no longer wore his bracelet, and she was sure that he'd noticed—not that she cared. During her enforced stay in the hospital, she'd had a lot of time to think, and one doubt had been plaguing her. "How come so many people were out to get you?"

Ash shrugged. "I've wondered that myself. I suppose fame makes for an easy target."

"Okay. Then tell me one other thing. Did you honestly write 'Only Raining'?"

Charley saw the answer in his eyes before Ash even replied.

"Yes . . ." he began, before looking away from her withering glare and admitting, "most of it."

He sighed heavily. "I had a verse but no chorus. Brandon Mills wrote the chorus. And he would've been credited if he hadn't cheated on Kay. He hit her too. Brandon wasn't a nice guy. So Kay literally wrote him out of the song. Her revenge. She swore me to secrecy. You see, Kay was building a story around me as this genius singer-songwriter. We had to protect the legend."

Charley nodded, accepting it without judgment.

"I wrote *all* of 'Angel Without Wings,' though," Ash was quick to point out. "And it's better than any song I've ever recorded."

He reached out to take her hand again, but this time she refused to take it.

"Charley," he said, "I'm donating all the royalties from this song into a recovery fund for you."

Charley was briefly at a loss for words. Then she snapped, "I'm not a charity case! Don't pity me!"

"I'm not," he replied, his tone wounded. "I just want to help you."

"Then leave me alone." Charley turned her head away and stared resolutely out of the window.

"No, you're my muse, remember? My inspiration. I have to take care of y—"

"I said, *LEAVE ME ALONE!*"

Stunned by her hostile reaction, Ash sat motionless for a full minute, then stood up. "If that's what you really want, Charley. But I won't abandon you. The song is yours. The money too. And if one day it can help you walk, then it'll be the greatest song ever written."

With a longing last look at her, Ash left the room.

When he was gone, Charley sobbed her heart out. Why was she pushing away the only person she truly cared for?

But she already knew the answer. Ash reminded her too much of all that she'd lost.

Through tear-filled eyes, she saw an update blink on her phone: FILE DOWNLOADED.

Slipping on her headphones and pressing Play, Charley listened to the song—*her* song—and wept . . .

44

"Why here in particular?" asked Jason, pushing her wheelchair down the boardwalk of San Clemente pier. "There are other beaches far closer."

"I used to surf here," replied Charley sadly. "Used to."

Foaming white breakers rolled in like familiar friends along the sandy strip of coast. But they passed her by on the pier, like they'd forgotten who she was, no longer recognizing her.

And who'd blame them? She was paralyzed, in a chair.

Charley watched a young girl with blond hair catch a wave and ride it all the way in. It could so easily have been her. But surfing was just a pipe dream now. Like everything else in her broken life, nothing was simple or easy anymore. Just taking this trip down to the beach had been a mission. Climbing out of bed, going to the bathroom, putting on clothes, getting in and out of the car, negotiating the path, even making it up the shallow incline to the pier.

It had been one major challenge after another. On this, her first excursion into the outside world, Charley was confronted by all the things she used to do effortlessly. Instead of celebrating her day out of the hospital, she just felt an aching sense of loss.

The sight of the surfer girl was the final straw.

She began to cry.

Jason stopped pushing her. "Hey, Charley, what's the matter?"

"I—I'm not meant to be trapped in a chair!" she sobbed. "I can't dress or wash myself or even go to the bathroom on my own. And I can't walk, can't surf—can't do anything! I can't stand another day of this. I simply don't have the strength!"

Jason knelt down beside her, placing a hand on her knee. She could feel it now—just.

"Charley," he said softly. "You have more strength and courage in your little finger than all of us boys together. What was it that philosopher said . . . ? *Whatever doesn't kill you makes you stronger.*"

"If that's true," she retorted through clenched teeth, "I should be stronger than reinforced steel!"

But she certainly didn't feel that way. Inside she felt as brittle and fragile as Styrofoam.

"You are," said Jason, his gaze unwavering. "You overcame everyone to be the best in bodyguard training. You overcame every threat in every assignment. And you will overcome this setback. Nothing has stopped you before. Why should this?"

Charley didn't answer him. Jason couldn't possibly understand what she was going through. Only those suddenly paralyzed could.

The two of them fell silent, and Jason continued pushing her along the pier, the wheels of her chair rattling over the wooden boards. Charley felt every bump and jerk as she sat immobilized, a prisoner in her chair. She was surprised and touched that Jason had made the effort to visit her. But she was also stung that Blake hadn't come—he'd sent her a get-well card, but that was it. Jason had been right. She was better off without him . . . better off without anyone.

"I hear once you're fit, Colonel Black's asked you to return and head up Alpha team," he said casually as they reached the end of the pier. "I think that would be good for you. Give you a focus. Have you thought about it?"

Charley gave a barely perceptible shrug.

"For what it's worth, I've asked to be part of Alpha team if you take up the offer."

"What? So you can be my legs for me?" she said, more harshly than she intended.

"No," said Jason, brushing off the sting in her words. "Because I think you'd do a great job, with all your experience."

Charley glanced up at him. "I thought the colonel was going to put you in charge of your own squad."

"He was, but I want to be on the *best* team. Led by you."

"Listen, Jason, that's very flattering of you. And I appreciate you flying over to see me. But . . . can I have some time alone?"

"Sure," said Jason, flicking on the chair's brake. "I'll get us a drink."

As he headed back down the pier, Charley gazed out at the shimmering blue ocean. She studied the thin line of horizon that separated sea and sky and waited for the telltale ripple that would swell into the perfect wave to ride.

It wasn't long before a glistening ridge of sea rose up in the distance. Subtle at first but approaching with ever more promise. As the wave rolled toward the shoreline, Charley desperately wanted to jump in the water and surf her way in. But that was impossible.

IMPOSSIBLE . . . I'M POSSIBLE.

The opening to Ash's show flashed before her eyes, and a small voice in her head spoke up. *Who's to say you'll never surf again? It's only yourself putting up barriers.*

Charley pushed away the false seeds of hope. As the wave drew nearer, she took out the badge from her bag and clasped it in her palm: the gold winged shield of a guardian angel.

Who needs wings . . . to be an angel?

She'd come full circle. This was where her journey had begun—and where it would end.

She'd lost her best friend and her parents, and now the use of her legs. What more could life take from her?

Charley drew back her arm to toss the badge into the sea, but stopped in midthrow. She stared once more at the gleaming gold badge, then pinned it to her shirt. Fiercely, she flicked off the wheelchair brake and used the strength of her own arms to turn and roll herself back down the pier. One thought in her head . . .

We cannot change the cards we are dealt, just how we play the hand.

ACKNOWLEDGMENTS

My books have always included strong yet feminine heroines: Akiko and Miyuki in the Young Samurai series, Cho in my Ninja series, and of course Charley and Ling in my Bodyguard series. But *Target* and *Traitor* are my first opportunities to write entirely from the perspective of a female lead character . . . and what a heroine Charley proved to be! I hope you enjoyed reading her adventure as much as I did writing for her.

So, with Charley in mind, I'd like to thank all the women who have had a major influence in my life. First and foremost, my mum—thanks for all your support, love and sacrifice. I am blessed to have you as my mother. Next and equally as important, my beautiful wife, Sarah, and the mother of my two whirlwind sons, Zach and Leo—I truly appreciate all the patience, love and tenderness you show me and the boys. And of course my dear departed Nan—you gave me a head start, steered me in the right direction and left me with words of wisdom that will last a lifetime. Your light forever shines in my heart.

Karen, as you know, I consider you a sister—thank you for being there for me through thick and thin, joy and sadness, and being a constant friend in my life.

Sam Mole, my awesome sister-in-law! And Sue Mole, a dream of a mother-in-law!

The first book of Charley's adventure is dedicated to my gorgeous goddaughter, Lucinda Dyson. May you grow up strong, confident and happy. I'll always be there for you.

I'd also like to thank my friends Emma Gibbins, Hayley Drew, Katharine Ravetz, Alessia Sardella, Abbie Moore, Georgie Farmer, Fiona Findlater, Lisa Martin, Barbara Horsfield and Clare Hatfield—each of you have had a significant and positive influence on my life.

Then there's my Bodyguard squad at Puffin: Jessica Farrugia Sharples, Hannah Sidorjak, Wendy Shakespeare and Helen Gray.

And, finally, one person I must thank and who is an exception to the female rule: Brian Geffen, my awesome editor in the U.S.—I couldn't ask for a more enthusiastic, hardworking and dedicated editor. Keep up the good fight!

Stay safe,

Chris

Any fans can keep in touch with me and the progress of the Bodyguard series on my Facebook page or via the website at www.bodyguard-books.com.